W9-BZV-359

THE ADVENTURES OF JOHN CARSON IN SEVERAL QUARTERS OF THE WORLD

THE ADVENTURES OF JOHN CARSON IN SEVERAL QUARTERS OF THE WORLD

A NOVEL OF ROBERT LOUIS STEVENSON

BRIAN DOYLE

ST. MARTIN'S PRESS
NEW YORK

THE ADVENTURES OF JOHN CARSON IN SEVERAL QUARTERS OF THE WORLD. Copyright © 2017 by Brian Doyle. All rights reserved. Printed in the United States of America. For information, address St. Martin's Press, 175 Fifth Avenue, New York, N.Y. 10010.

www.stmartins.com

DRAWINGS BY DENNIS CLEMMENS

Library of Congress Cataloging-in-Publication Data

Names: Doyle, Brian, 1956 November 6– author.
Title: The adventures of John Carson in several quarters of the world : a novel of Robert Louis Stevenson / Brian Doyle.
Description: New York : St. Martin's Press, 2017.
Identifiers: LCCN 2016043274| ISBN 9781250100528 (hardback) | ISBN 9781250100535 (e-book)
Subjects: LCSH: Stevenson, Robert Louis, 1850–1894—Fiction. | Authors—Fiction. | San Francisco (Calif.)—Social life and customs—19th century—Fiction. | BISAC: FICTION / Literary. | FICTION / Historical. | FICTION / Biographical. | GSAFD: Biographical fiction. | Adventure fiction. | Historical fiction.
Classification: LCC PS3604.O9547 A63 2017 | DDC 813/.6—dc23
LC record available at https://lccn.loc.gov/2016043274

Our books may be purchased in bulk for promotional, educational, or business use. Please contact your local bookseller or the Macmillan Corporate and Premium Sales Department at 1-800-221-7945, extension 5442, or by e-mail at MacmillanSpecialMarkets@macmillan.com.

First Edition: March 2017

10 9 8 7 6 5 4 3 2 1

For Mary

608 Bush Street

Preface

From late December 1879 until April 1880, before his marriage on May 19, Robert Louis Stevenson lived in a rooming house at 608 Bush Street in San Francisco. Tall, thin, poor, cheerful, young (he was twenty-nine), and hopelessly in love with Miss Frances Matilda Vandegrift Osbourne, originally from Indianapolis but then a resident of Oakland, Stevenson spent his days roaming the sprawling legendary city by the bay, spending miserly sums on food and half a bottle of wine per night, and writing furiously to try to make enough money to support the family he would instantly have when married; Fanny already had two living children by her profligately adulterous husband, from whom she was finally divorced on December 15.

Stevenson worked up his notes from his travels across America, which became his book *Across the Plains*. He worked on a novella, which became his book *Prince Otto*. He wrote a dozen essays, at least, and various small articles for local newspapers. Missing his native Scotland, he worked on an autobiography, never published. He wrote poems, notably the famous requiem that would be engraved on his Samoan gravestone in 1894.

And he contemplated a novel, to be called *Adventures of John Carson in Several Quarters of the World,* perhaps based on the stories of his Irish landlady's husband or brother-in-law. He may not have even started it; no scrap of draft or sketch or notes has ever surfaced, and no intent scholar has traced the mysterious John Carson; but ever since I read about this unwritten book of Stevenson's, many years ago, I have dreamed about writing it for him.

It is an inchoate urge and I cannot easily articulate the reasons it so appeals to me. Something of celebration of a man by all accounts honest and kind and generous; something like rising to the delicious bait of a challenge; something of a detective story, perhaps, beginning with the sparsest of clues, ten words on which to build castles and ramparts and swirling depths of story; something like gentle homage to the writer of verve and dash whom I admire above all other writers in my language; something of a love song to one of the great American cities; and something surely of pure happy curiosity—to begin a story on a foggy street in San Francisco, many years ago, and see where in the world we might go . . . !

—BRIAN DOYLE

Any story, as soon as it is spoken aloud, is a true story.

—JOHN CARSON

Thin-legged, thin-chested, slight unspeakably,
Bold-lipped, rich-tinted, mutable as the sea,
The brown eyes radiant with vivacity—
There shines a brilliant and romantic grace,
A spirit intense and rare, with trace on trace
Of passion, impudence, and energy.

—WILLIAM HENLEY, ON ROBERT LOUIS STEVENSON

My taste runs to hourglasses, maps, seventeenth-century
typefaces, etymologies, the taste of coffee, and the prose of
Robert Louis Stevenson.

—JORGE LUIS BORGES

Pure poetic eloquence (colored always, be it remembered, by a
strong Scottish accent), grave argument and criticism, riotous
streaks of fancy, flashes of nonsense more illuminating than
wisdom, streamed from him inexhaustibly as he kindled with
delight at the delight of his hearers . . .'til all of us seemed to
catch something of his own gift and inspiration. As long as he
was there you kept discovering with delight unexpected powers
in yourself. . . . He was a fellow of infinite and unrestrained jest
and yet of infinite earnest, the one very often a mask for the
other; a poet, an artist, an adventurer; a man beset by fleshly
frailties, and despite his infirm health, of strong appetites
and unchecked curiosities; and yet a profoundly sincere
moralist.

—SIR SIDNEY COLVIN, ON ROBERT LOUIS STEVENSON

I MET JOHN CARSON FOR THE FIRST TIME on Bush Street in San Francisco, where I was at the time living in a rooming house owned by his wife, Mary Carson. Though born in Ireland, Mary had for some time been a citizen of The City, as she called our rough and misty citadel, as if it was a ship upon the water; which in truth it was, for a few streets west lay the Pacific Ocean, and a few streets east sprawled its impatient bay, like a tiny dinghy bobbing alongside a tremendous parent. To further the image, Mrs Carson's house, tall and thin, stood at the apex of a hill, and swayed like a mast in the afternoon wind, and often featured a sort of sea-beacon at its peak—the night-lamp in my room, where I scribbled the remarkable stories I heard during the day from Mary's husband John.

I was then a penurious man, forced to be so by circumstance, and I had much time on my hands, waiting for a marital entanglement to unbraid itself across the bay, and free the woman who would be my wife; and while I walked the city as much as I could, having learned that cities are best discovered on foot, I also had the open hours and eager ears for Carson's adventures, for he was a terrific teller of tales, and spoke in such a colorful and piercing way, with such adornments of elocution and wonderful mimicry, that whole afternoons passed as unnoticed as the tide, as we sat by the sitting-room fire.

He had been everywhere and done everything, it seemed, and he was eager to tell of countries and peoples, crimes and misdemeanors, mendicants and millionaires, and all the manners of living he had seen, from high to low and every shade between; and while Mrs Carson would occasionally offer tart reproof and call him to task about one detail or another, his flow was never stanched, so long as I was there to listen, and later record what he had said, in prose as close as I could get to the way in which he had said it; for he had an essentially riverine style of speaking, and his reminiscence would wander into pools and oxbows, there to swirl meditatively awhile before returning eventually to the main stem of the story. But then other times he spoke so speedily that you were rushed headlong through the narrative rapids, before being released at last into a placid stretch, there to slowly regain your equilibrium, and smile with pleasure at the unforgettable rush of the voyage.

*

I had arrived at Mrs Carson's estimable house in December of the year 1879, and spent the latter half of that month recovering from illness, essentially confined to my attic room, and in little contact with the other residents except for the solicitous Mrs Carson, who was kind enough to bring me small sustenance, and what books she could find unclaimed in the house; during that time I much enjoyed Mr Twain's *Roughing It* and *Tom Sawyer,* and Mr Whitman's new *Leaves of Grass,* and a steady run of excellent books by Mr Henry James, whom I had met in England and very much liked, though he seemed far more English than American to me, and, I suspect, to himself.

Having long been in poor health I was all too familiar with the land of counterpane, and was used to spending my ill hours in bed, writing. I was then by trade a scribbler, a writer of slight essays and occasional pieces for the newspapers, and it was to the hunting of this small game that I devoted my energies that wet December; not until after the new year did I improve enough to shakily go downstairs and sit by the fire, and then stroll the neighborhood, and finally wander the towered salty city itself, from wharves to hilltop thickets and back again. From January to April, then, I roamed as freely as the fog in what proved to be one of the most turbulent and riveting cities I had ever seen—fully as lovely and avaricious as Paris, as arrogant and fascinating as London, as windswept and grim and prim and delightful as my own native Edinburgh. And of those pedestrian journeys there is much to tell; but my most memorable travels in San Francisco that spring were all conducted in a deep chair by the fire in Mrs Carson's house, as I sat mesmerized by the estimable Mr John Carson, gentleman and adventurer.

★

I should begin by showing you the man, insofar as I am able, as he was then, at the prime of life and the peak of his powers. Taller than not, and burly rather than thick; as he said himself, while we saw eye to eye as regards our height, he was twice the man I was in volume. A dense head of hair, just beginning to silver at the temples; clean rough clothes somewhere between the utilitarian garb of a sailor and the unadorned simplicity of a reverend; boots that were worn but buffed, boots that had seen something of the world but would never allow themselves to appear in public with stain or scuff. No watch fob, no necktie, no hat; I once remarked to him that I had never once seen him in a hat, and he laughed and said he thought most hats were affectations and aggrandizements, very much like the useless showy feathers that certain birds developed in order to lure unsuspecting females into their sensual bowers; the only hat he had ever worn and liked was a helmet, which had done its work well, and protected him from a shower of blows, any one of which would have been sufficient to make Mrs Carson a widow.

His face was like his clothing, rough but honest and open; no beard, by the express command of Mrs Carson, who disapproved of beards in general as disguises, and disapproved of his in particular as a brambly barrier between man and wife; and as he said with a smile, what sensible man, graced with the affections of the extraordinary Mrs Carson, would fail to do everything he could to encourage and fan those affections?

Sharp amused eyes, of a gray-green color, like the bay in

mottled weather; dense eyebrows as thick as bushy caterpillars; large rough hands I would see at work around the house, carpentering this and that; as he often said, to build a house of mere innocent wood, and expect it to withstand a week of San Francisco's weather unscarred, was the airiest folly; it was no accident that Our Lord spent eighteen years apprenticing as a carpenter, for surely the Holy Family was planning to move to San Francisco, where Our Lord would have been able to carve a good living from a career of household woodworking.

An unadorned voice, neither mellifluous nor harsh; his voice was like the man, direct and amused but capable of sharp turns and dangerous calms. A tiny tattoo of a falcon below his left ear, less than an inch long, noticeable only in crisp daylight. A man of measured tastes in food and drink, well read but not scholarly, sociable but not gregarious or garrulous. An aficionado of music, but none that I had ever heard; by his own account he loved the music of lands far away, the aboriginal music of Borneo and Australia in particular, and he rued his lack of instrumental skill, he said, for he would have liked to have that music drifting around the house, reminding him of his travels and his friends in far-flung regions of the world.

He was fond of gently teasing Mrs Carson, and gravely proposing fanciful adventures and enterprises to her, such as purchasing one of the Seal Rocks islands off San Francisco, and building a ship upon it, in such a way that the rough surface of the island was completely covered by the ship, so that while in residence there husband and wife would always be at sea, but never in danger of foundering; or that they erect such a collection of stalwart canvas sails on the roof of their house, that in high winds they could sail north to redwood country for the day, or south to Half Moon Bay, there to wreak joyous havoc among the oysters when it came time for dinner.

Indeed there were so many of these speculative invitations to Mrs Carson, two and three a day sometimes, that in my first weeks in the house I thought him perhaps slightly unhinged, or even politely inebriated, but soon I came to see that the custom was something of a coded conversation or verbal waltz between two people who much enjoyed each other's company. I think now that I learned a great deal about marriage from John and Mary Carson, of Bush Street in San Francisco; for in my own marriage I have especially appreciated humor as a crucial virtue, and have seen for myself, perhaps too often, that wry wordplay and gentle jest are not only nutritious but sometimes the very seed of salvation.

*

Mrs Carson's house, I have said, not Mr Carson's, or the Carsons' collectively; and that is a good place to let Mr Carson begin his story, for the house was not only the port and refuge to which Mr Carson returned again and again after his adventures, but the sweet old chapel of pine and oak, as he said, where he had courted "the extraordinary landlady," and been married, in the sitting room, by the fire, by a priest with whom he had served in the War Between the States. So let us begin by that sitting-room fire, on a thoroughly moist day, early in the year 1880, as Mr Carson carries us back in time, to the year of our Lord 1864.

I had just asked him how he met the extraordinary Mrs Carson, and so we begin:

"That was a year after a legendary San Franciscan dog named Lazarus had died and did *not* manage to come back to life, despite several days of close attention by the newspapers to a possible miracle," said Mr Carson from his chair on the other side of the fire. "October; I remember that your fellow ink-man Mark Twain was a reporter for *The Daily Morning Call,* and that he wrote a memorable article about

visiting Lazarus's grave in the Odd Fellows Cemetery, and waiting there quite a long time for the dog to be true to his name, to no avail. *I* thought the article was amusing, but Mr Twain was soon gone from the newspaper staff, for unspecified reasons. I suppose he left so as to pursue his literary career, but I have always savored the notion that certain segments of city society were affronted by his lighthearted speculation about Lazarus rising from his grave in the Odd Fellows and floating over Lone Mountain, the mercy of the Lord having been profligately poured upon even so meek a citizen as old Lazarus, who was a disreputable creature, as I remember, although a very fine rat catcher.

"I had met Mr Twain that spring, when he arrived from Nevada, where he had been a silver miner and a newspaperman, often reporting from Carson City, from which he speculated all Carsons came, perhaps hatched from tremendous pinecones and then set loose upon the world; indeed perhaps we were manufactured by seasons, he said, with Johns and Bills sprouting in spring and the Jims and Bobs arriving en masse in the fall, and the new females surging up the Truckee River by the thousands, more Susans in an hour than a man could count in a day.

"He was full of colorful ideas like that, and not loath to share them with you or anyone else; you never met a more cheerful headlong fellow in your life, and while some of his free talk earned him the threat of fisticuffs, not once in the time I knew him did anyone actually set about inflicting corrections on his person. But beneath the high spirits there was a darker man, as is so often the case with the publicly humorous. I saw that side of him here and there, when he was in his cups. But he was the sort of man that when most down on his luck was most generous and free; I remember when he discovered that his whole bulging trunk of silver mining stocks, which he had thought worth thousands of dollars, were not now worth a thousand cents, he laughed and took me to a dinner featuring a hill of oysters and a river of beer.

"The last I saw him was on this very street, down the hill toward the bay. He told me he was off to try mining again, this time for gold in the Sierras, because he had not a dollar to his name and must leave the city, but he would give me a tip worth more than Astor and Carnegie and Vanderbilt together, because he valued our friendship with all his soul, and would always remember that I was a true friend when he was down and dark and needed a grip and a grin to haul him from his dark crevasse. Up the hill there, he said, pointing to this very house, there is a building which I believe will loom large in your life. Do not ask me how I know such a thing. I do not know myself. I am a man of dreams and portents. I sometimes suspect I am a magnet for such things. There is Scotland and Wales and Acadia in my family tree, which may explain a certain predilection to omens and spirits. Also somewhere back a ways I have an ancestor named Ezekiel, who may have known the Biblical prophet himself, and lent a certain necromantic cast to the line ever after. Probably they ran a tavern together, or schemed to defraud the pharaoh of his crown. Who can explain these things? Not me. But trust me when I say that you and that willowy house up there will some-day meet, and the auspices seem beneficent. So, John, this is farewell, for I don't know when I will be back in the city, or whether we will meet again in Tahiti or Timbuktu; but I have given you the treasure of a lifetime, I believe, with this advice, and I hope with all my heart that someday I will hear of your happiness, and know that for once I did a good turn by a friend, who did so many good turns for me.

"And off he went," said Carson, smiling at the memory of his friend. "I heard later that he had gone to the Sand-wich Islands, and then around the world, and now he is a famous man, resident in a castle in Connecticut, he says; I had a note from him recently, with a copy of his newest book; our postman was much amused by the address, which was simply 'John Carson, Bush Street, San Francisco, Where He Lives in That Tall Skinny House, If He Had Any Sense or Imagination at All.'"

"And did you," I asked Mr Carson, "turn on your heel that day, and walk right up the street to the house?"

"Oh, no," said Mr Carson. "No, I did not, for ephemeral reasons—I think I was hungry, and down to the docks I went for oysters and beer. No, Mr Stevenson, I walked east that day on Bush Street instead of west, downhill instead of up, and there were many strange adventures before the mo-ment that I did finally knock on the front door of this house, and discover that my life was changed from that moment

forward, to my great surprise, and eternal pleasure, and endless gratitude."

★

That night, when I went upstairs to jot down this story, I
realized that John Carson had not actually answered my
question, and explained how and when he met Mrs Carson;
and I was soon to discover that he was wonderfully deft at
evading the skeletal facts of a story, especially that prized one,
even as he was irresistibly fascinating at detailing the evoca-
tions and shadowy corners of a tale. No man I ever met was
as riveting a storyteller in the matter of its moods and intimations, its scents and sounds; when John Carson told a story
you were soon inside the story yourself, your feet on the
sands of a beach in Borneo, your hands snatching at a fish in
an Australian sea, your eyes scanning a ridgeline for enemy
cannon emplacements; indeed after some long afternoons
with John Carson by the fireplace I would climb the stairs to
my room as tired as if it had been me walking miles through
a pitiless jungle, or rowing from one end of a remote bay to
another through sheets of rain, or salving and sewing the
wounds of my friends by a guttering candle all night long—
all things that John Carson had done, in several quarters of
the world, when he was young.

Where was he born? He never did say; but he often spoke
with great reverence and affection of Scotland, and the names
of certain towns and rivers there tumbled familiarly off his
tongue—Dalbeattie, Wigtown, Portpatrick, Kirkcudbright,
the River Nith, the River Cree. It seemed to me that he

must have had cousins at least in that western corner of Scotland, if not closer relations, for he would occasionally speak of his "people" in Caledonia, the old name for Scotland; he steadfastly refused to use English names and labels for anything, and grew sharp-tongued whenever he heard the phrases *Great Britain* or *British Empire*—"there is no such thing as Great Britain, only one country enslaving its three immediate neighbors, and much of the rest of the world, and to even acknowledge an empire is to acquiesce to its imperial murderous greed"—thus John Carson, in the rare moments when he was annoyed or angry.

Those moments were few; I never met a more equable man, or one more willing to listen to someone else's questions and inquiries and speculations; and he was the welcome sort of man whose attentiveness drew you out, welcomed your own anecdotes and tales, sparked your own conversational liquidity; so that sometimes I would arrest my own flow of talk, and realize that I had been talking for fully twenty or thirty minutes uninterrupted, with John Carson hanging on every word, and not waiting impatiently to interrupt, or turn the line of talk toward his own experience, or denigrate or supersede mine, as so often happens between parties who are less conversational than oppositional, or merely taking turns as monologuists.

Now, I have met some wondrous talkers in my day, some mesmerizing storytellers, genius sculptors of the spoken word, male and female, young and old, from the glens of Scotland to the craggy mountains of France, from the streets of London to the endless plains of America, and some of them, I suppose, have been so riveting and unforgettable in tone and cadence that their voices have soaked into me unawares, and been born anew in the voices of characters in my pages; yet John Carson was a new species to me, for I sat with him for weeks and weeks on a regular basis, and heard the whole spill and swirl of his life in his inimitable telling, a tremendous outpouring, over four absorbing months; it was as if I was at the university of the man, studying biography and personality and theatrical flair, history and geography and psychology all at once, and all under the one tutor, who was by turns exacting, and airy as a child on the shore of the sea. Some days he would spend an hour detailing a monumental single moment from his past; other days he would sprint through a whole year in that selfsame hour, and toss off such tantalizing casual bait as "that man wore a suit of crocodile skin," or "I was then offered the daughter to wed, but declined"— but then never return to that corner of the story, however strenuously I tried to bend him back in that direction.

When I was a child in Edinburgh I had a nurse, Miss Cunningham, whom I loved with all my heart, and who was the first fine storyteller I knew; in her case it was not only tales from the King James Bible, that glory of muscular literature, from which she read aloud with a voice that encompassed all weathers in the telling, but also a limitless parade of stories of haunts and ghosts, of terrors and glowering mysteries, at which I quailed but which I loved, in that strange way we human beings do, to want more of the very thing that makes your hairs prickle with a delighted horror; and then in my own jaunts and voyages I seemed to meet more than my fair share of wonderful raconteurs, all of whom appealed to me greatly, and not only for the zest and entertainment of their tales, but because the invention and spinning of a fine story seemed like the greatest of joyful labors to me. Something in tales and telling sang to me, in ways that the engineering of lighthouses, or the dreary practice of the law, never had, or could; so there may have been no more ready or rapt listener in the world for Mr John Carson, when he sat down by the fire in the dawn of the year 1880 to tell me of his tumultuous life; and perhaps there was no storyteller of more immediate and lasting effect on my life and work subsequently than that estimable San Franciscan, whose voice I can still faintly hear sometimes, in full and headlong flow, on certain days when the wind is up, and the windows are a-rattle, and the fire is ticking low. Even now, many years and miles from that tall mast of a house, I will hear him for a moment, and be thrilled again, and remember the pleasure of his company, and the zest of his tales, and the warmth with which he spoke of his friends, some of which he did not expect to ever see again in this life, but whom he savored and esteemed for their courage and kindness, counting himself the luckiest of men, to have had such companions for a part of his road.

*

The first adventure he told me complete, from beginning to end, with a proper setting-forth and returning-home, was his time in Borneo, in the year 1854, when he was not yet twenty, he said, and "wholly unattached, footloose and wandering wide, with neither a penny nor a worry to weigh me down; I felt then that no one cared for me and so I cared for no one, and so I did throw myself headlong into situations that a more sensible man would have avoided, or tiptoed gingerly around such scrapes; but not me, not then.

"How I got to Borneo is of no consequence; it was, of course, by ship, a long story in itself for another afternoon, perhaps, for that was a savage ship, and I was never so relieved in life as to be gone from it finally. Suffice it to say that I found myself on the coast of Sarawak, at the tail end of that year, and while I spoke none of the local languages, I could *work,* the language that needs no words; and soon I found myself upriver on the docks as a laborer, loading and unloading ships and boats during the day, and acting as a warehouse guard for a local merchant at night. Though ostensibly Sarawak was at peace that year, after years of savagery among various tribes and interests, piracy was not uncommon, and even a boy as young as me was welcome as a sentinel, or first to fall under attack, more likely. Also the merchant believed me somehow to be a soldier of fortune, though I had never claimed such a thing, and so he paid me to defend his interests at night against the pirates.

"I have not told you, though, of the scents and sights of Borneo then, the immediacy of jungle and mud and river and insectry; the many kinds of monkeys in the trees, leaping with astonishing skill from branch to branch, and chattering like so many high-spirited small boys; the fishing nets everywhere hung out to dry, and the palm-thatched houses of every conceivable size from sturdy house to tiny hut; and mud everywhere in every color of the rainbow from bright gold to the bleakest black; and alligators, and ants, and satinwood trees, and gardenias of breathtaking size and allure—you could smell them from a mile away, it seemed to me, and even now I will be stopped in the street occasionally by a gardenia calling to me from some distant window; another language without words, I suppose, the inexplicable wonders of scent. This happened to me a week ago Tuesday on Mission Street and for a moment I was absolutely sure a flower from Sarawak had seen me passing below and called to me, with a sudden cry of recognition, as a sister would to a brother she had not seen in years, and had not expected to see again in this life; but I could not find the source of the scent, and walked home saddened, and inarticulate, when it came time to explain my long face to Mrs Carson.

"The sun-snakes, the flower-snakes, the mighty cobra-snakes, some as long as eight or ten feet, and terrifying indeed when they reared broodingly up, as tall as a man; and the boa-snakes, big enough to eat deer; many was the man who told me stories of snakes so big you could hardly believe them possible still on this earth, and of unlucky people who vanished into the maws of boa-snakes, and of tribes in the mountains who could live for a month on the meat of a single snake, were they lucky enough to capture one of the old chieftains of that race.

"And the birds!—so very many birds of so very many

species! Trying to make some sense of their variegation and relationships and cousinly pattern was how I came to meet Mr Wallace. There was the crocodile-bird, with a song like a thrush, and pigeons and parrots of every color, cuckoos and kingfishers, and ten kinds of eagle, two of whom dearly loved to eat snakes above all else. And all sorts of plovers and terns and stilts along the shore, and owls and swifts and wood-peckers in the forest, and what seemed like a thousand tiny songbirds of the warbler type, elusive as dreams among the fronds; my favorites of all of these were called sunbirds, tiny gleaming creatures that did indeed shine and glitter most amazingly, as if they had bathed every morning in the life-giving orb itself, and shimmered with its aura the rest of the day until dark, at which point they too subsided and van-ished until tomorrow's resurrection.

"For two months, October and November, I lived in a shed near the docks, a tiny structure that had long been used for curing tobacco, the scent of which was so powerful that Mrs Carson says she smells it upon me yet, although she may be joking. Curiously I was not lonely, for during the day I was so busy, and so thrown into the tumult of people and commerce, that in the evenings it was sweet to lie at rest, and smoke a pipe, and listen to the orchestras of birds at dusk, before go-ing off to my night-work at the warehouse; *that* job was the lonely one, for I was by myself, and could not sleep for fear of being overpowered by the pirates, who were famous for their silence at night, and were said to be able to approach even the most cautious wild animals unawares, which they would do

in training for their marauding. But while I could not sleep, and was anxious of incipient violence, and armed myself with knife and stick, I could fill the hours with contemplation of the myriad birds, and begin to draw them, and compare their structure and style of life one with another, to try to see some pattern in their profligacy; how did the eagles and hawk-owls differ, for example, in what they sought as prey, and how did they go about killing their daily fare? Did the one specialize in fish, and the other in small animals? How came the serpent-eagles to be so good at capturing that elusive food, and other eagles to choose another diet altogether?

"It was by chance I met Mr Wallace, who had sought

among the natives for men and boys especially interested in local fauna to serve him as guides for the explorations he had planned into the wild country. He had found such a lad, of fourteen or so years of age, named Adil, whose family I had come to know and esteem, and occasionally sup with, and play chess with the children, bright young creatures who had learned the game from their elders. Adil it was who introduced me to Mr Wallace, persuading that gentleman that I would be the perfect additional companion for their perambulations, being of strong body and able to translate something of the local languages, bits of which I had picked up on the docks; ever it has been the case that workers along the shores and beaches of the world are the quickest linguists, for the tidal wash is where all the languages of the world meet and compete, and a man there must be able to speak some of all, if he wishes to earn his bread and avoid being cheated. So it was that I had a little Malay, and Chinese, and Dutch, and even Dayak, for the warrior peoples of the interior did sometimes have concourse with the Malays and the Chinese, in between bouts of piratical endeavor.

"Mr Wallace had arrived in Sarawak on the first of November, at the invitation of the white rajah of those parts, the adventurer James Brooke, and he was for his first weeks in residence with the rajah, with whom he too played chess, and discussed natural history, and smoked cigars, and debated the possibility that great apes like the local orang-utangs were our ancestral cousins and even perhaps remnant ancestors. During the day, however, he and his young assistant Charles, who had accompanied him from England, would explore the river and environs, utterly absorbed by beetles and butterflies. Occasionally Adil and I would help in these local jaunts, during which Mr Wallace's energy was a most remarkable thing to see; he was perhaps thirty years old or so, and a lean and active man, and relentless in his pursuit of insects; also he was an indefatigable walker, quite capable of fifteen miles in a day, and there were days when all three of us with him on his expeditions arrived home bedraggled and exhausted, the boys to fall asleep instantly but myself off to duty at the warehouse.

"It was on one of these long expeditions into the forest that Adil was lost. Charles and Mr Wallace decided to go deeper into the jungle, toward the mountains, in pursuit of new species of butterflies that would, Mr Wallace believed, be nectaring on plants at higher elevations; Adil and I turned back toward home. It was late in the afternoon, and we were both weary, and I was not due for work on the docks for days, the ships being scarcer in December, the close of the rainy season; so as night fell, we made a fire, and ate a small supper, and fell asleep under a thicket of palm fronds.

"I awoke before dawn, as has been my lifelong habit, to discover Adil vanished. For a few moments I thought nothing of it, considering that he might be gathering fruit, or wood for the breakfast fire; but then I noticed bent and broken ferns, and realized that he had been hauled away through the underbrush, perhaps by a leopard, or even one of the sun-bears said to be common in these forests, though I had never seen one;

I had, however, seen lithe and powerful leopards, and knew them to be quite capable of capturing and killing a boy, whom they might consider a species of monkey.

"Perhaps I should have sprinted back down to town, and alerted the rajah and his people, who knew the whole country well, so that they could have mounted a search; but I did not. For one thing I liked the boy, a gentle soul, and was infuriated that he might be endangered, and me asleep while he was taken; and for another I could not bear to waste another minute between disappearance and pursuit; and also it seemed to me the trail was patently clear and evident before me, so that I could not turn away and walk in the other direction. So it was I set out after Adil through the trackless forests, armed with a knife and desperation.

"I suppose this sounds like a foolish quest now, that a boy of nineteen would leap into the dense forest in pursuit of a boy of fourteen, possibly taken by a leopard who would no doubt adamantly defend his prey; not to mention the myriad other dangers of that jungle, and the fact that I knew nothing of the country beyond the main trail along the river; but I was young, and angry, and afraid, and those are powerful engines of our actions, as you know very well yourself— you who journeyed through a hundred miles of remote mountains with no companion but a donkey, as you told me, and that just two years ago, so it is still fresh in your mind, and maybe on your boots, and in the moist spots in your coat that will never fully dry.

"The trail was clear enough where Adil had been carried

through the jungle, and I followed it all morning without a break, hurrying as silently as I could, watching out for dangers; I was afraid in particular of the many snakes, and often stepped into a thicket with my heart in my mouth. Early in the afternoon I found a spot where Adil and his captor or captors had stopped awhile by a stream; and here I examined the ground closely, to see if he had been hurt, and what manner of being had stolen him from our night-fire. I could find only the prints of human feet—two men, it seemed to me, of about the same weight and stature—and while there were signs of Adil supine and probably bound, there was no blood, or evidence of harm.

"Where Adil had lain, though, I noticed shavings of wood, as if someone had been carving or working wood, perhaps for a fire, though I found no ashes or embers. The shavings were fresh; but I could find no hint of the sticks, and I guessed that they had accompanied the fugitives, perhaps as weapons, or walking sticks of some sort.

"On I went until dusk; and then I found the most remarkable objects, cunningly placed in a tree bole in such a way that a man of my height would have to notice and remark them as he stopped to choose between two divergent trails. Of all the things you would expect to find in the deepest forest of that densely jungled island, two roughly hewn chess pieces are perhaps the last; yet there they were, two small knights, fresh-cut from palm, and staring out at me from a shelf in a tree. In an instant I realized that Adil had left them for me, and was perhaps telling me that he had been taken by two warriors; and my heart sank, for the only warriors in Sarawak who did not fight for the rajah were the men of the Dayak, the fearsome aboriginals who had battled the Dutch and English colonists for years, and swept down on merchant shipping with a terrible ferocity, and who fought the rajah as he sought with equal ferocity to expunge their piracy from the local waters.

"Now I *was* afraid, for men are more savage than leopards and bears, who only wish to eat, or defend themselves, whereas men are violent for a thousand reasons, many of them beyond all understanding; but I pressed on, all night, walking as cautiously as I could, and looking closely for any other markers Adil might have left. By remarkable chance the night was clear and lit silvery by the moon. All around me were the cries of animals on the hunt or being hunted, a sea of sound I sometimes hear even now on the wildest winter days here, when everything is wind-whipped and the gulls especially shrill; but none assaulted me, though several times I surprised something large, which leapt away with a crash, and probably thought me a new sort of night terror inflicted on the innocent woods.

"I found a pawn, and then another, and then a third, and considered that Adil was trying to leave me a chess piece at roughly the same intervals. Then I found a castle, or rook; and this one caused me pause, for it was very hurriedly made, much more so than the others, and it seemed to me there was a splash of blood in the well of the castle. Perhaps Adil had cut himself, in his haste, or perhaps it was just a splash of rusty rain; in any event I took the message to be that he was arriving at a camp or stronghold of some sort, and I would be well advised to double my caution. A few moments later I came to the edge of a clearing in the forest, and discovered exactly such an encampment, roughly fortified by logs and poles. Though I could see no sentinel or patrollers, I could hear the bustle of it, and see campfire smoke rising against the first straggle of dawn; and I sat down there in the fringe of the forest to consider what to do."

Just then Mrs Carson entered the sitting room, and called us to dinner, and John Carson immediately rose to go; he laughed aloud at me sitting gaping in my chair, feeling abandoned, so to speak, and teetering on the precipitous peak of the story. "When Mrs Carson invites you to dinner," he said with a smile, "you are wise to accept her invitation with alacrity, for her gifts in the kitchen are as legion as the rest of her virtues, and I can report from sad experience that the other guests in the house will not wait for the table-tardy, nor leave a scrap of savory for anyone who lingers by the fire. Plus it would not do to be anything but instant when Mrs Carson has offered a gift, which is what you have to call her wonderful productions. As for the story it can wait for us to return to it; stories are patient, as you know better than I do, having written books, and the story will be right here when we return to it apace." And away he strode to dinner, with me a step behind, marveling at the subtle pleasure of a story paused in full flow, the delicious tension of waiting; and after dinner I was happily inundated by memories of my beloved childhood nurse Cummy telling me stories in stages, a bit every night, as you would parcel out the most delicious candy.

2

SAN FRANCISCO IN WINTER IS A CITY of lashing rain and swirling mist, the two often interchangeable and indistinguishable; but sometimes after a day of rain the sun would beam forth so generously that it almost seemed to stack itself in drifts in the street. On those days especially I walked the city with a most sincere pleasure and curiosity, for never was there a city so precipitously hilly, so graced with odd and unusual domiciles, and so bravely lax in the basic principles of architectural engineering. I saw houses built into the most alarmingly unsuitable and unstable places, fitted into their peculiar footprints with far more hope than cement, it seemed to me; and there were rickety houses built on pillars thin as stilts, and rooms built over sheds already grossly overburdened, and houses built at such fearsome angles on hilltops and cliff faces that one epic sneeze inside would topple all and sundry in an instant; yet only once did I see the ruins of a fallen house, and that one caused by a political explosion rather than structural sin, or so it was reported in the newspapers.

Up and up I went, always up, it seemed to me, and many times I wondered how this could be possible, that I would always be climbing up, always be rising, as it were, and never in decline; yet this seemed so, and some days I would return to Bush Street happily weary and exhilarated from several hours of uphill work, and stop to think that somewhere in the world a man surely had done the other part of my walk, his perambulation being all down the steep stones of his city, so that we had accomplished several miles, myself on the rise and himself in descent, together enjoying a most bracing afternoon.

My favorite walk was up Telegraph Hill, which had been called Signal Hill in years past, for from it a man could easily spy all the ships coming into port, and signal their arrival to interested parties, so as to advance their commercial chances. This seemed to me the steepest of all San Franciscan hills, so much so that grass grew in the streets, because no horse or cart could climb such a pitch; residents and visitors alike maneuvered on wooden stairs and steps, which wandered in such profusion that it seemed a very heaven for carpenters and woodworkers, who must be always at work here, given the debilitating effect of the winter rains. Perhaps because it was so hard to climb, the hill seemed populated largely by immigrants from Italy and Spain and Portugal, and their musical languages were everywhere to be heard, reminding me of certain neighborhoods in London; and here too, more than anywhere else in the city that I knew, were the tiny balconies of crowded cities in the Old

World, where men sat and smoked and chaffed their neighbors, and women hung their washing and called to their friends on balconies above and below. I never wearied of walking those precipitous streets, which always seemed filled with cheerful banter and the faint redolence of newly sawn wood; to me it seemed like a village unto itself, the top of Telegraph Hill, with its own culture and mosaic of languages, and its residents instantly out on their balconies to bask, if the sun should appear shyly after rain.

January 5, 1880, Oakland

Dearest Louis,

I snatch a moment to write a letter even though you
will be here tomorrow, for I am sunshine after rain,
I am dawn after dark, I am spring born of winter! Free
of *him* and open to you, free to love, free to plunge into
a life that will take us who knows where . . . I cannot
find the words, Louis. I cannot find the words! I sit and
smile in the garden and sweet little Lloyd comes to sit
with me and feel my brow to see if I am sick, for he has
rarely seen me smile, poor boy.

Free of him, free of him!—three weeks I am free of
him now, after the final decree on December 15, and
I confess, Louis, that I take the document out of its pine
box sometimes, the tiny coffin of that terrible marriage,
and stare at it in disbelief, in awe, in amazement, in
relief, incredulous. A piece of paper that frees me forever
from his oily smile and easy lie, the scents of a hundred

women, his utter lack of care for his own children! He
did not weep, *he did not weep,* when poor Hervey died,
only six years old, my poor baby coughing his life away
into a towel, a blood-soaked towel, I washed so many
towels, Louis, I washed so many towels!—if I could get
all the blood out of the towel then Hervey would
recover, he would be healed!—but I couldn't get them
clean, I couldn't, though I tried so hard, and he died,
poor little Hervey. Isobel washed his body and combed
his hair and dressed him in his best suit. She was seventeen.
The same age I was when I married the dashing
lieutenant. Lucifer! It was a blue suit with narrow lapels
and Lloyd gave him his own best boots. Lloyd was just
eight years old then. He loved those boots. You know
how a child loves his things and hoards them and talks
to them. Hervey was always asking to wear those boots
and Lloyd would say no and they would argue like shrill
jays but I watched Lloyd tiptoe in and put the boots
onto Hervey's feet that night before the funeral. I saw
that happen. As you say there are more stories of power
and grace available than we could see and hear were we
given a thousand more eyes and ears and years. I miss
you so. I will make the finest dinner anyone ever made,
tomorrow—and there will be flowers, though it is
January—and Lloyd wants to start a newspaper with
you—you will be the wise and freehanded publisher and
he will be the brilliant editor and reporter and pressman
all rolled into one—we will be by the cottage door

waiting with open arms when we hear the ferry coming tomorrow—my life, my very heart!

Your loving,
Fanny

I was in Oakland for the next two days, and missed my hours with John Carson telling stories by the fire, but on the eighth of January, the feast day of our Scots compatriot Saint Nachlan of Aberdeenshire, we sat down again to the sitting room, in the afternoon, and I begged him to tell me what had happened to Adil, and what manner of people had carried him off, and why.

"You will remember that I arrived at the village before dawn," said Mr Carson, "so that I had some time to formulate a plan, and to contemplate the village as it awakened. As the sun rose I realized that here before me was a settlement of the Dayak people, famed for their warlike nature and for their ancient custom of collecting and preserving the heads of their enemies. While most of the other residents of the island regarded the Dayak with terror, those who fought them could admire their courage and tenacity in, as the rajah said, essentially defending their ancestral lands, just as we would, confronted by people who would take away our land and our ancient means of life; and while it was Brooke who was famous for defeating them at sea, and reducing their piratical assaults nearly completely, it was also Brooke who could be most eloquent and passionate about their qualities and virtues, as he understood them to be.

"I stood there in the fringe of the forest for a long time, trying to envision how I might approach the village without being captured or killed, or slip into it unannounced to find Adil, but it was a knotty problem, for the place was well fortified, and I could see the outlines of sentinels here and there. But then in a sense the forest whispered an idea to me, and wild as it sounded, the sheer brass of it made it appealing, and just possible as a means of pacific entry to the Dayak village.

"I have not explained sufficiently the extraordinary lushness of the flowers in the deep jungles of Sarawak; and all around me, as I stood there behind a tree, I realized there were flowers of every conceivable sort and shape—orchids of a dozen colors, rhododendrons of many shades of rose and lilac, flowers of the vinous plant Ixora, which seem to stretch for miles sometimes amid the halls of the trees. In a trice I was adorned with flowers from head to foot, with only my eyes and mouth undisguised; and, screwing up my nerve, for I was well aware that this was either a brilliant stroke or my final steps upon this earth, I walked out of the forest and toward what I took to be the main entrance to the village.

"In many cultures there is an exception made from the norm for the holy fool, the peaceable jester, the solitary clown, the harmless soul who capers and japes, and is looked upon with a gentle eye by the populace, as you would look upon a small child, innocent and incapable of danger; indeed perhaps some of our general latitude with hermits and tinkers and street prophets and wandering minstrels is a reverence and affection for the child so patent in them and so reduced in us; I have often thought, watching people offer alms to buskers, that perhaps the urge is not so much generosity as it is a subtle melancholy for the time when they too rambled as airy and unworried as birds; the years when you were young, and not yet absorbed by business and battle, and able to be footloose and improvident, and hope for occasional kindness like a beam of sunlight in an otherwise dreary day.

"I was in luck; the sentinels, while suspicious and rough, did not run me through, or remove my head to be boiled, but brought me to their chief. This man was a most remark-able fellow, in several ways. First was his appearance, which was unlike anyone I had ever seen. He was tattooed from the crown of his head to his waist, in fantastic images of animals and birds and divine beings; even his face was thoroughly tattooed with astonishing attention to detail, so that if you stood closely you could see intricate details of leopard claws, the mottled leopard of the remote hills being his particular patron and divine companion, as I was to discover later.

"Second was his dwelling place, which was raised high above the forest floor by poles as thick as mature trees, and covered everywhere by a jacket of the most exquisitely over-lapped and woven leaves, so that his tree house, or airy castle, was proof against the constant rain and mist. Inside were the skins of bears and buffalo in wild profusion, hung from the walls and laid out on the floor, so that anywhere you sat was dense and warm. All along the walls was a collection of swords and knives and spears as numerous and bristling as the weapon-room of any warrior in the world; and he could wield a sword with skill and ferocity, too, as he showed me several times, slicing apart fat chunks of wood with ease, and once reducing a small deer carcass to pieces for the pot with several lightning strokes, almost faster than my eye could follow.

"Third, and most surprising, he had snippets of several languages, and could even distinguish among Australian and Scottish and English accents; he also knew bits of Chinese and Hollandish, and apparently much of the other native dialects of the island; how he came by all this linguistic facility I never knew, though I would give much even today to hear that story; now *there* would be one of the novels you so wish to write.

"I will call him Lang Labang, the Pale Hawk in his language, for that was his nickname or walking-name, as the phrase was among those people; to use a person's true name was not permitted, and only your confessor and most intimate loved ones even knew your inner name, which could be spoken only in moments of the greatest need, when a door needed to be opened between this world and the next. Names had great power among those people, and even to this day I find that I pay much more attention to their use and dignity, and never myself mouth them casually anymore, preferring to use honorifics in the daily ramble, where possible; thus you will hear Mrs Carson and me refer to each other that way in public, and that is why it is more comfortable for me to call you Mr Stevenson than anything else you would prefer, given our growing friendship. Perhaps someday we will use our deeper names. Sometimes I wonder if we all do not have not two or three names but ten or twenty, depending on who we are by the hour; for we are many different men during the day, let alone a year, or a life. Dark and light, wry and bitter, generous and mean, gracious and violent; we might even go so far as to say that we are good and evil by turns, the two battling constantly in our souls, and the face a man presents the world is only the placid surface of a pool all a-swirl in ways even he cannot fully understand.

"But to return to the story: Lang Labang did indeed hold sway over Adil's fate, for the boy had been taken as a captive, the Dayaks disliking the Malays intensely, over many ancient feuds, and attacking them wherever and whenever they had the chance; this was the reason for their sea-piracy, against which Rajah Brooke had fought so fiercely, and now had much reduced, with a ferocity equivalent or surpassing theirs. However the Dayaks had continued their war against the Malays in other ways, and would capture and enslave any Malay they could. Thus two men of the village, noticing a Malay boy deep in the forest, determined to capture him, and did so silently when we were asleep. Adil was safe for the moment, I was informed, but his fate was set, for the Dayak had no concept of ransom or exchange of prisoners, or returning a captive for future considerations.

"But Lang Labang was a very perceptive fellow, and it is his sharp eye and quick intelligence that Adil can thank for his freedom. In interviewing me about my tracking of Adil, and my work for Mr Wallace, and Mr Wallace's close friendship with the rajah, he had pieced together the story of the chess pieces left as signals for me along the trail; and with a great roar of pleasure he produced a chessboard from a vault behind the furs, and set it up on what appeared to be a large jar, or drum of some sort. Soon enough I was given to understand that he knew and loved the ancient game, had learned it who knows how, and was always in search of opponents against whom to try his steel; it was one of his ambitions in life to someday play a game of chess with Rajah Brooke himself, for whom he seemed to bear no ill will, saying that the rajah's war against the Dayaks was against the sea-Dayaks, not the people of the deep forest, and as he well knew himself the sea-Dayaks were in general a scurrilous and untrustworthy people, and not the sort of clansmen he would be at pains to defend.

"The good Lord alone knows what fancy possessed Lang Labang that day, but it was a lucky day for young Adil, for the chieftain's proposal to me was a chess game for the life of the boy, one game to determine his fate: freedom if I won, slavery and early death if he won. For a moment I hesitated, wondering if I should propose best two of three, considering that I knew nothing of my opponent's skill, or if I should plead another case, considering the lunacy of betting a child's life on the outcome of a game; but, looking around at the glowering guards, and realizing that the peculiar offer might be withdrawn at any moment and the boy and perhaps myself imprisoned or worse, I accepted the challenge, and we commenced to play.

"I do not think I could explain the strange tension of the next hour, if I had a week to try to tell it. The grim stalwart guards brooding in their corners, alert to my every gesture, ready to run me through without a second thought, did they think me a danger to their chief. The silent man across from me, his tattooed face sunk in his tattooed hands as his mind ranged the battered chessboard, his earrings and bracelets glinting in the shafts of sunlight from the door, his heavy necklaces slacking gently when he leaned in to contemplate the board more closely. The ever-so-slight rippling of the furs on the walls, and the creaking of the vegetative structure itself, and faintly the voices and sounds of the villagers at their daily labors; the sudden yelp of a dog, a happy shout to a friend, the tart snap of a mother admonishing a child. During the game there was a sudden shower of rain, all of a minute long, rattling against the tree house; and once I thought I heard a piercing scream in the distance; an animal being slain, it seemed to me, or the cry of the legendary orang-utang of these forests, but I could not be sure.

"I never played more slowly and thoughtfully than I did that day. I hesitated over every move, and stared long at the patterns and possibilities before I committed my hand, as did my opponent; it was almost like the boy Adil sat there between us, mesmerized by the game also, and more than once

I thought I could nearly see his face in the air over the board; a most unsettling feeling, and not one that eased my mind or sharpened my play.

"I do not know who it was who taught that man to play the game of kings, but howsoever he learned it he had learned it well, and he played with startling confidence and command. Within the first few moves he had me on my heels, and it took nearly an hour for me to battle back to a position of strength, from which I could try to pin his king into a corner prison. He fought wonderfully, constantly sending his horsemen in particular on spectacular sallies, essentially alone; and while I could not but admire the singular vision and energy of these adventures, and myself expend much effort fending them away, still, they did not advance his cause, and after another hour his king and courtiers were forced to the wall, with their stubborn foot soldiers falling one by one to slow but relentless assault.

"I do not know if the Dayak way with chess is never to concede a game, or if that was his personal creed or custom, but the chieftain would not or could not cede the battle before its appointed end; but finally that moment approached, and he laid himself open for what he knew was the final blow. I remember that he then sat back, and looked me full in the face for a long moment, and I him, before I reached out to finish things. It is a subtle pleasure of chess that the pain of loss, in a well-played game, is essentially shared by both players, for he who is to win has been inside the mind of his counterpart for an hour or more, and feels the sigh, if not the sting, of defeat;

there is almost a sadness, at the conclusion of a fine game, that one must win and the other lose, for there has been a curious intimacy of mind, an exploration and appreciation of each other's style of thought, and creativity, and resilience, and when the game ends it is almost the case that each man must struggle back up to the surface of the quotidian.

"I made my move, and finished the game, and we sat there silent for a moment, over that scarred old chessboard of unimaginable provenance; and then the chieftain gestured with his hand, and the guards went to retrieve the boy. Lang Labang then led me outside, and very soon I found myself outside the settlement with Adil, myself still adorned with a multitude of flowers, and the boy harrowed and drawn from his travails. As we made our way through the forest over the next day he told me haltingly of his capture, and how he had been rushed through the forest, twice being carried bodily when his captors felt that he was deliberately slowing their progress, and how he had hoped and prayed I would see and understand his messages, and how, when the guards had come to release him, they had ceremonially "killed" him with their swords, and then restored him to life with water poured from their shields, so that his two captors would be reimbursed properly for the loss of their property, but himself freed to return to his own people, under my protection, by command of the Pale Hawk, whose authority in this part of Sarawak was unquestioned.

"Curiously I saw Adil only once after this adventure, and that from a distance, as I took ship to leave Sarawak some weeks later; he was on the beach, and our eyes met for an instant, but then he was obscured by passersby, and I saw him no more, though I have often thought of him over the years, and wondered at the shape of his life, and what he tells his own children of his brief sojourn among the forest-Dayak, and how it may be said that the ancient game of chess saved him from being enslaved. But I have not seen him since nor do I expect to, though I wish him well, and sometimes think with pleasure of the look on his face that day, when he saw me in the Dayak village, standing with the chieftain, and realized that he was free, and walked with me through the pillars of the stockade and into the jungle.

"I did stay in correspondence with Mr Wallace, however, and you being a learned man will know of his subsequent achievements and feats. A most remarkable man, Mr Wallace—famous for his thinking along evolutionary lines, and for a general acuity of scholarship and authorial excellence; but to me the measure of the man is his curiosity—you never met a man more genuinely interested in people and animals and plants and humor and spirituality and life than Mr Wallace, and without the slightest condescension or high and mighty attitude about his intellect and his tremendous learning. Also the sheer animal *energy* of the man was amazing, and him not what you would call a prepossessing physical specimen; yet he could walk all day through the forest, and climb any crag or alp, and indeed he rattled up the tallest trees as quick as a leopard, chasing after his beloved butterflies and flying-frogs; many was the time we would be walking along, Mr Wallace and Adil and me, and I would be terrifying Adil with a story about the fifty-foot snake seen in this vicinity, and suddenly Mr Wallace would be galloping up a tree as quick as can be, having seen a certain beetle, or an unknown orchid, or the huge black butterfly he subsequently named for his friend the rajah. A wonderful man, always kind and generous. We stay in touch yet, with the occasional letter, and he sends me copies of his books—Mrs Carson and I particularly cherish his book about the Malay archipelago, though much of it concerns his work there after we parted company. We persist in hoping that someday he will, in his travels giving lectures, see fit to visit San Francisco; this is a clear possibility, he says, for he has a brother in California whom he has not seen for years, and he says he would be delighted to walk with us in the hills, as we did in the old days. I would not be surprised, though he must be nearly sixty years of age now, to see him scramble up one of our redwoods or sequoias, and there discover four new species of insects in four minutes, and then produce a small owl wholly new to science."

He paused, and cocked an ear toward the kitchen, and smiled, and offered to bet me a dime that Mrs Carson would be calling us in to dinner in one minute exactly, for he had heard a certain signature rattle of crockery indicating the imminence of sustenance; and I realized with a start that here we were sitting by the fire in the rooming house, and that darkness had fallen outside, and we were not, as every iota of my being had thought we were, in the sweltering jungles of Sarawak, gaping as Mr Alfred Wallace ran up a tree with the grace of a cat, having seen an orang-utang, and wishing to procure it for close study of its tremendous upper musculature, thrice that of the strongest man!

Mrs Carson did call us in to dine, and Mr Carson preceded me to the table, but I lingered for a moment by the fire, savoring the wonderful feeling of having been absolutely and completely *transported* by his story. Now, I have heard many fine storytellers at work in my travels, in many corners of the Old World and New, and I count myself fairly well read, and so apprised of magical tellers of tales on paper, but never could I recall such an *immediacy* of story as this, in which I was genuinely startled to be called back to the present, from being so plunged into an adventure. Mr Carson, using only his voice emerging from the darkness, had composed a whole and complete world, and populated it with people I could see and hear and touch, and had drawn me in with such skill and depth that I *felt* the oppressive tropical heat of Borneo, and the rough handling by Dayak guards, and the fearful tension of that shadowy chess match, on which hung the life of a terrified boy cowering in a hut; indeed I thought I could faintly smell the suit of fragrant flowers he had worn as he walked out of the forest. That such a level of tale-telling was possible! But my moment of contemplation was here truncated by the scent of roasted chickens and fresh-baked bread; and as I am twice as hungry as there are hours in the day, and Mrs Carson a cook of surpassing and capacious talents, in I went to table, to enjoy the weekly feast to which I am entitled as a boarder, and which I would not miss for all the kings in Christendom. But all the rest of that night I reveled in what I had learned was possible in this bruised and tumultuous world; that a man could tell a tale so riveting that time and space fell away altogether, so that when the story paused or ended, the listener—or the reader!—would be snapped awake as if from the most delicious dream, and would have to shake himself or herself for a few minutes, as you shake away the bright fading threads of dreams. And in both cases there is a subtle sadness, that you have been called back to this life from a most alluring voyage, as well as a subtle pleasure for which we do not yet have good words, that you were so riveted and absorbed by the tale; and I vowed that night, back upstairs at my writing desk, to aim in future for this very thing that John Carson showed to me, one day by the fire, in San Francisco, on the feast of Saint Nachlan of Aberdeenshire, beloved of Scots.

3

MY SITUATION WITH MISS FRANCES MATILDA VANDEGRIFT
Osbourne, originally of Indianapolis but now resident in
Oakland, across the bay from my tower on Bush Street,
was loving and painful at once, during those opening months
of the year. While we were very much in love, and in full
and delighted agreement as to our future together, and in
my readiness to share the care of her two children (Lloyd,
aged eleven, and Isobel, aged twenty-one, and just married
to a painter), we were also wholly at sea financially. Her wastrel husband Samuel, lieutenant in the United States Army but
a renowned general among the philanderers of the world,
had finally agreed to be divorced in December, but had not
yet legally granted Fanny the house in which she lived, nor
a shilling of any other assets or support, so that she was essentially penniless, and depended upon the alacrity of my pen
for her sustenance and that of the children.

As for myself I was recovering from a long illness in Monterey, from which I had finally fled to San Francisco; I was at
odds with my parents in Scotland, who did not wish me to

marry Fanny, and so withheld any and all financial assistance; I was dependent upon my friends in England and Scotland to sell such essays and stories as I could provide, to periodicals and publishers there, as I knew nothing of the American market, or if there even was such a thing, for such slight ephemera as I could hastily compose; Fanny's family in Indiana had not been apprised of her divorce, nor of the lewd and egregious cause of it, for fear that an emotionally fragile sister or two would dissolve wholly at the news, and evanesce on the spot; therefore her family did not know of her impending marriage to a penniless Scottish wraith, who sometimes seems more composed of cough than flesh, and appears to subsist on a diet of sunlight and cigarette smoke, the latter wrapped in two fat slices of the former.

Yet we were eager and fervid to be married, Fanny and I, in those months, and I would meet her once or twice a week at the ferry dock, and welcome her to my hilly abode with open arms, and we would walk to dinner with such a warmth of feeling that I had never experienced before, nor had she; for she had married the dashing Lieutenant Osbourne when she was all of seventeen years old, and had cause to regret her rash action within a month, she said—by which time she was carrying the infant Isobel, and could not, in good conscience, leave even a detestable marriage, if it would render her daughter fatherless—though the lieutenant proved to be as poor a father as he was a husband, having no time for wife or daughter, but all the time in the world for whiskey and women, and not in that order.

Usually Fanny and I repaired to Bush Street; not to Mrs Carson's house—I would not stain the reputation of either admirable woman with rumor—but to a restaurant I knew between Dupont and Kearny streets, where two frugal diners could eat as one, and share half a bottle of wine, and linger over their coffee, before the lady must be back on her bay boat, and home to her children, soon to be my children also; and then back up the steep streets I went, from the ferry pier through the shadow and swirl of the old city, to my seaman's berth in the timbered tower, and so back to work, writing as fast and furious as the muse would allow.

It was no sort of life, that life, but I had no choice in it, for Fanny had to wait for legal title to her house before we could marry, and I waited desperately for the daily mail, in which there might be ten pounds, if fate had smiled on me—or dunnage, if fate was grim; and I could not in good conscience have offered to marry her if I had nothing with which to support wife and children. I calculated that particular cost again and again, at my meager desk, and concluded that even with a wholesale trimming of our sails I would need two hundred pounds a year to float a family. Thus in my first weeks on Bush Street I worked on a book about my travels in America; I worked on a potboiler about swordsmen and thieves and mountebanks in old France; I worked on three or five or seven essays and articles at once, all designed for instant sale upon completion; but the latter briefer pieces stole time from the former substantive ones, and the books could not earn me a farthing until they were finished and away in flight toward amenable editors; and so I sat in my tower every morning, noon, and night, writing and writing on both sorts of things alternately; except for the hours that I sat with Mr John Carson, hearing his adventures in several quarters of the world.

There are times now, when I think of those hours by the fire with John Carson, that I believe I was saved by his stories; that what kept me from a real and deep and perhaps irretrievable despair was the daily prospect of tales from a master teller. I had little money, and little food, and little prospects of more of those necessaries; the woman I loved with all my heart lived away across the water, never knowing when she would be free to marry me; the children I would come to love as my own were away in the mist too, neither knowing when they would for the first time welcome a father who loved and esteemed and attended to them, like their first father had never done; and my own family and friends were even further away, and their efforts on my behalf either fruitless or frustrated. Many was the morning I awoke weary and dark, and many the night I fell asleep wearier and darker; but I did have one sort of wonderful food in prospect, a source of light, a beacon of hope and pleasure almost always available. So that when I tell you that I would break from my work late in the afternoon, as the winter sun declined and the wind freshened, and go downstairs for a cup of tea by the fire, and find Mr Carson there, having just added fresh logs to the blaze, my heart veritably leapt, for I knew I would instantly be plunged into an expedition unlike any I had ever known, and be kept from the hounds of worry and despair by this most discerning and witty fox.

It was in just this way in which Mr Carson began the story of his adventures off the wild west coast of Ireland; I remember the opening of this story particularly, for I had asked him again how he met Mrs Carson, and he leaned back in his chair, and was silent awhile—it seemed to me he was overcome by some powerful emotion—and then he began.

★

"I was twenty-two years of age," said Mr Carson, "and again had been aboard a ship for a time, this time in the wild Atlantic, and it came into my head to be ashore for a while, and savor good sturdy rock beneath my feet—not farmland or woodland or beach or bog, but crags and peaks, pillars and moraines, cliff faces and empty places. Why such a whim should possess me then I cannot remember, and perhaps did not know even then; your twenties are the years when a man wends and wanders, searching for who knows what—we say money or love or adventure, but I think those are words we invent to drape reason on the unreasonable. Suffice it to say that I departed my ship in a busy Irish port, but found that city in the throes of smoke and riot, and so I wandered west, until I came to an island so craggy and windy and lonely that I remember laughing aloud with the pleasure of it; I had found exactly where I wished to be, though I had not the faintest idea why I should so wish to visit.

"Now, I knew nothing of this island, or of the surrounding country, and so I had no idea why it was so empty, and seemingly brooding with sadness; I was there some days before I discovered that the island, and the county, and indeed the whole country had been crushed with famine for twelve long years, with no end in sight. So there were very few people on the island at all, and those few weary and bedraggled, and in no mood to befriend or even talk much to a foreigner, Celtic cousin though he be. A few dozens lived along the shores here and there, in protected coves, collecting seaweed and shellfish, and setting out hurriedly to fish in their small black boats when there was the rare break in the weather; you never saw a wilder weather than that island endured, for even on bright clear days there was wind enough to knock a man over and send him tumbling, as I more than once saw for myself.

"I had wanted rock, and rock I found there, for while some of the island seemed to be bog or beach or what the natives called *machair,* or grass-pasture, the rest was stark crag with hardly a path or trail anywhere. The whole western end was one tremendous mountain, made of a hundred hills, all shouldered up against the sea, and thoroughly lashed day and night by the wind, which was so strong there that the few trees were small and bent and crouched and huddled in the most amazing fashion in crevices and cracks. The greatest of these massive hills were Cruachán and Mionnán, but it was the third mountain on the island, called Sliabh Mór, that began to fascinate me, for on its south flank there was a village built wholly of stone, with nary a soul in it. The islanders would go nowhere near it on any grounds, for reasons

they would not tell; and after I had been on the island a couple of weeks I knew enough not to inquire further, for these were people concerned only with keeping life in their children, after the horrors of their recent past and uneasy present—for their potatoes still would not grow in the diseased plots, the sheep and cattle that had once been common were terribly reduced, the oats and rye formerly grown wherever decent soil was sheltered by the wind were hardly to be found, and even the uncountable fish in the profligate sea were very often saved from capture by the savagery of the sea.

"I had come to the island on a whim, to salve a personal sore, but young and selfish as I was, even I soon saw that I must be of assistance where I could; so I worked here and there in the villages, or what remained of them, and I lent my small marine expertise to the fishing boats when the sea was calm enough to venture out after silvery food; and I can say that I was of some help in the fishing, for I was young and strong and knew what I was about, in pursuit of cod and salmon and herring and even seals, and the tremendous placid sharks there, who were easily caught and did not fight, being of some peaceable species I did not know.

"It was fishing with one family in the westernmost village, called Dumha Acha, or 'sand-bank,' that led me finally to the stone village I had often wondered at from afar. The old man of that family, whom I had thought to be a grandfather or older but had turned out to be the father, only forty years old but withered and worn by the awful years, told me about the stone village one night. It had once been a vigorous settlement, made by men gifted with stone, who built in the old ways, small round cottages that fended off the wind; but then after the hunger struck, the village was abandoned, and the people in it moved together down to the shore, where they might find fish and weed to eat. There were those who might tell me that the stone village was then used as a 'booley,' or summer camp for people bringing their animals up onto the mountain for the grass, but this was not so, and the truth was that no one would go near it now for any reason; it was a place of sadness, without even a name; one story he had heard was that the name had been buried there too, along with the dead from the hunger, and now no one called it anything but the village on the mountain, when they referred to it at all.

"I inquired as to the people who had lived here and he said they were all gone, that even the survivors who had come down to the sea were dead or gone to America, and that was the sum and total of what he or anyone else alive on the island knew about the village. It was a measure of how deep the sadness was, he said, that there were now no stories whatsoever of the people there and their lives, their joys and works, their particular heroes and saints and sinners; and his advice to me was that I was better off leaving the dead place in peace, for the mountain to reclaim in its own time. The mountain was patient and would eventually reach for its stone children, and erase all sign and memory of men in that place.

"But somehow I found that rather than be discouraged from going there, I was twice as eager as before; and off I went before dawn, climbing through mist and first light, pausing here and there only to marvel at the vistas that opened before me, and be glad that there was no rain and only small winds. In the afternoon I finally came to the village.

"I suppose there were a hundred or more stone cottages there, and they were of all sizes and shapes, although most of them were small. Most of them, too, it seemed to me, had arrangements by which animals could be sheltered both inside and out, and many had their larger entrance on the east side, which I speculated must have been the quieter side for the wind. All of them, or all of the ones I examined carefully, were wonderfully constructed with stones of every conceivable size placed exactly so as to support and strengthen each other. Indeed I was so fascinated by the stone-mastery that I almost missed the crucial detail that is the essence of my story.

"I was particularly absorbed by the smallest of the cabins, those with no windows and apparently no recesses for fireplaces or sleeping-quarters; I wondered if these had been set aside for certain people, or used simply for storing goods and tools against the weather. I was examining the interior stonework of one of these at the west end of the village, near a stream, when I found, behind a loose rock in a niche, a pot and a small knife. For a moment I thought these someone's lost treasures, hidden and then forgotten in the leaving; but then I noticed that the pot was not at all old, and the knife was razor-sharp. Could it be that the village had one last resident, or that someone had come upon it, as I had, and decided to stay?

"By now it was full dark, and the prospect of climbing back down the mountain was uninviting, and also I wondered if the mysterious resident was necessarily friendly; so I slipped out of the hut and hid myself, resolving to watch and wait, and see if I might glimpse whoever it was who used the cabin, and perhaps returned there every night. Here my years at sea served me well, for I had learned long ago how to stay awake for hours at a time, alone and quiet, alert to any change, and it was no hardship for me to sit still—and at least here there was no chance of being swept overboard by a sudden gale.

"I waited a very long time, it seemed to me, and then finally my vigilance was rewarded, perhaps an hour before dawn. I saw a slight movement, something that was no owl or prowling fox; and then the something dimly became a person, though I could not discern anything of age or sex. Whatever person this was slipped silently into the hut with the pot and knife, and did not immediately return.

"This put me in a pretty position—I could surprise the inhabitant, and perhaps receive that knife amidships, or I could slip away, trusting my own stealth; but now I was powerfully curious, and I decided to announce myself. You must remember here, Mr Stevenson, that I was all of twenty-two years of age then, and as full of undue confidence in my own strength as any preening stripling is; not until we have been in a few battles do we begin to suspect that we are rarely the cock of the walk, and far more often the sacrificial fowl.

"Neither was I a fool, though, and my time at sea and in Sarawak had taught me some caution and care in moments like this. So I armed myself with some stones, and took a deep breath, and slid out of my hut and toward the other, as silently as I could go. The sun had just risen behind the shoulder of the mountain, and there was the faintest new light among the huts; I remember that detail in particular, for I did not want to be silhouetted in the doorway, and so be made an easier target for assault. I hesitated an instant, there by the door of the other hut, with my arm cocked to deliver David's pebble against Goliath of Gath—when, to my absolute astonishment out of the hut walked . . . a girl!"

Just as John Carson uttered that word, and I startled with surprise, Mrs Carson called from the kitchen that dinner was served, and no delay whatsoever would be tolerated this evening, for tonight we were granted her rabbit stew, on which she had lavished hours of effort, and it should be eaten steaming from the pot, and it *would* most certainly be eaten steaming from the pot, with steaming hunks of her extraordinary bread also, or we would henceforth be shifting for ourselves in the kitchen, God save us all from such a tragedy. And in we went to the kitchen, John Carson and me, prompt as can be, though I had a hundred questions in my mouth about the girl; but it says something of our affection and respect for Mrs Carson, and for her incredible culinary skills, that neither of us even considered anything but seating ourselves as swiftly as possible at that lovely old kitchen table, and partaking of Mary Carson's legendary rabbit stew.

*

Again the press of personal matters kept me from the fireplace at Mrs Carson's for a couple of days, though many was the moment, as I walked the hills with Fanny, planning our lives together if Providence was merciful and fate conspired to allow our joy, that I went over that fraught scene in my mind, and saw John Carson gaping, as out of the round stone hut on that wild mountainside came a girl. . . . Who was she? What was she doing there, where no other human soul lived for miles? What was the fabric of her being, the tenor of her soul, how did she earn her bread? It was curious, how much I found myself thinking of a girl in a story that was not mine; how ironic, to be furiously writing stories myself (and I cannot now emphasize enough how dire the financial situation was, and how energetically I composed, for the wolf was past the door and breathing savagely at my neck, could I

not hurriedly and instantly write stories both true and invented, as if there is much difference, if any, between the
two), but be actively yearning to hear the end of another
man's story!

But the chance did come, and it came at a happy hour for
me, for I had enjoyed a rare productive burst lasting most of
a day, and nearly finished my book about my travels across
America. I had come to a natural stopping point, and stepped
out onto Bush Street to stretch my legs with a walk before
dinner, when coming up the hill at a brisk clip I found Mr
John Carson, with the selfsame idea; so off we went together,
on a route he much enjoyed for the array of maritime vistas
it provided—up Kearny Street to Telegraph Hill, and then
west along Filbert Street to Russian Hill, from which you
can see and smell all the great waters that cup and assault
the city, and have done so since long before there was a being of our kind here, and it was all the province of deer and
hawks and bears.

Mr Carson was, I should say, a relentless walker, and
though we walked long that day, up and down the long
sinewy streets and finally back down Hyde Street toward a
much-anticipated dinner, to him it was a jaunt, who had
many times, so he said, walked from one side of the city to
another—usually down Geary to the sea, to which he was
still unconsciously drawn, though his seafaring days were
behind him. Indeed, he said, more than once he had gone
for a walk before breakfast, just to savor the bracing air, and
seemingly a moment later found himself on the beach, a clear

four miles from his home; but Mrs Carson knew and understood his inevitable tides, and only smiled when he reap-
peared just in time for lunch.

But our long walk that day is memorable to me also for
this: that Mr Carson resumed his tale of the stone village on
the wild Irish mountainside, as we walked, and I will relate
what I remember of it here, asking only that you must imagine hearing it told on the move, the late-afternoon winds
growing stronger as we go, until they blew as strong and
salty as the winds on Sliabh Mór, many years ago when John
Carson was a tall boy at the door of a hut, and out walked a
girl whose face, he said, he saw in his dreams even today.

"She *did* have the knife in her hand," he began, "and I
thanked my stars that I had not leapt through that doorway,
for there is no question she would have plunged it into my
neck, quick as a hawk impales a rabbit, and that would have
been the end of the very short story of my life. But she held
her hand, and I held mine—partly from a mutual astonishment, I think, but partly also from sheer curiosity; each of
us wondering how on earth the other had arrived at this
moment in this remote place.

"By some mysterious agency we established a truce, and
agreed to parley; and so imagine this, if you can: a young
man and a young woman sitting cross-legged amid the pale
worn stones at dawn, gesturing and gesticulating the stories
of their lives to each other, for neither of us had a word of
the other's tongue, and there is no common ground between
languages hatched on different islands. She spoke the Gaelic

of her people, and me a sort of English, I suppose, although it was English shaped to a Scottish mouth, which has no love for the place where that imperial and imperious tongue was born.

"But, as you know, there is much that can be communicated without words, and we had a wonderful conversation of the hands and fingers, and even arms and legs. At one point I told her of my shipping experiences by imitating a tilting deck, and roaring a storm in my throat; similarly she told me of burying her people by digging their graves in the air, and kneeling over their stony tombs, and weeping until she was dry. I told her of pursuing Adil through the jungles of Sarawak, brushing aside creepers and fronds with my arms, and myself being a leopard slipping away silently through the understory; her fingers set snares for hares, and her hand was the throttled coney, headed for the pot, and both her hands picked imaginary bilberries, and bearberries for medicine, and snapped the necks of the occasional unwary goose or duck; she even showed me how she would occasionally catch and roast the tiny brown lizards among the rocks, although she also was silently eloquent about how poorly they tasted, and how hungry you must be to eat such bits of bitter meat.

"In another man's story," continued John Carson, "there would be mention of her name, and her age, and her beauty or lack thereof, and her lissome appearance, or not, but I have nothing to say of these things, for what struck me most powerfully was the force of her personality, and what I could only assume was indeed her remarkable character; for as far as

I could tell from her stories, she had lived alone in the abandoned village for something like three years, hiding easily from the occasional visitor, as anyone climbing to the village could be seen approaching long before he arrived. She knew the mountain better than any eagle or fox, and knew every nest, every den, every berry bush, every secret cave; indeed, from what I understood, she had secret bolt-holes in several places on the mountain, and could move from one to another like a wraith if necessary; twice it seemed that official parties had searched through the village, either police or soldiers, for she remembered their uniforms, although she knew nothing of their origin, or purpose.

"We sat there by the doorway of the hut from dawn to noon, conversing with our hands, not even essaying words at all after a few awkward early tries, and believe me when I say that I never had a more riveting morning in all my life. Part of it, I suppose, was the sheer oddity of the scene— among the pale stone cabins long shorn of their residents, high on the shoulder of a remote mountain, far beyond the reach or sight or sound of any other human being for many miles around. The occasional cry or song of a bird, and once the slash of a fox against a straggle of bushes, probably headlong after a hare; once I thought I heard an otter at work in the creek that divided the village into two parts; several times the piercing whistle of a hawk overhead; but otherwise only the wind, and very faintly the murmur of the sea to the east, the west, the north; and all those small sounds themselves the faintest background to the astonishing theater of the girl sitting among the stones.

"It was about noon when our silent conversation came to an end, as I say; she indicated that she must be up and about on business, and you will understand something of her clarion will when I say that it did not occur to me to disagree, or insist that she accompany me back down to the flatlands, or invite myself to accompany her on her rounds. And too I felt very much that this was her ground, her home, her place and not mine, and she had been wonderfully generous to me with her time, and had not assaulted me, or fled from me, or called down the wrath of the mountainous spirits on an outlander, but instead had been clear and confident in her discourse. Indeed her calm sense of herself was what appealed to me most about the girl; however strange her circumstance, living there alone among the whispering stones, and however haunting and horrifying her past, during which everyone she loved had withered and died in the most awful manner imaginable, still she lived, and lived with a certain brass and brio. Not for her the slough of despond, the swamp of despair; nor did she, that I noticed then or after, feel the slightest sorrow for *herself,* that such trial and terror had been her lot. She *lived,* do you know what I mean? She was alive, and eager, and vibrant, and vigorous, and cared not a fig for what the world thought, or ostensibly owed her; her whole being was bent to being alive, with no time left over for philosophy; and I will say that I found this refreshing, as if she was a trickle of clear delicious water in a place where no such thing seemed at all possible.

"So off she went, up into the crags of Sliabh Mór, where the eagles for whom the island is named had their unreachable nests, and down I went, back down to the sea, and a few days later back *on* the sea, in yet another ship. I had made her one promise, that I would tell no soul of her presence in the abandoned village, and neither speak nor write of her life, which she preferred to live unheeded; and I kept that promise too, until now, though I found myself thinking of her often, and wondering if she was well. But here we are at home, Mr Stevenson!, and if I am not mistaken we have timed our arrival perfectly, for that, my friend, is the irresistible scent of roasted ducks, and there are no hands on this earth as deft with ducks as those of Mrs Carson. To the table as fast as we can go, and you will see that there is a meal even more delicious than her rabbit, and that is her duck, with sauces and drippings that London will never know, and Paris only imagine, and no man explain, not even such an author as you, sir, for the words for such extraordinary tastes and flavors have not yet been coined."

And so to dinner we went, and it was every bit as savory as he had claimed; and it was much later, when I was abed and just beginning to dream, that I realized again that he had not answered my question about how he met Mrs Carson . . . or had he?

4

BY THE END OF JANUARY my own affairs were in slightly better order—essays were off to editors, stories away to publishers, my health somewhat improved, Fanny's annual winter illness in decline, her two children—*my* two children!—well, and here and there the wet winter relieved by a sunny afternoon, as bracing as a brandy on Sunday; and one afternoon I found myself in the kitchen of the house, listening to the admirable Mrs Carson herself, who has not, in this poor chronicle, been given a single lonely page on which to speak on her own; so let us redress this oversight, and hear from her.

I had asked her the same question I had asked Mr Carson, how they *met,* and as her hands whirled and swirled to create our dinner (that night it was fresh herring, caught by Mr Carson that morning), she told me tales. And here I must interject, that in the same way no man could accurately describe her appearance, so no man could explain her voice, or the manner of her delivery; as close as I could come would be to say that when she spoke you were instantly *inside* the story she was telling, so that if she was speaking of the sea, you felt it seethe beneath your feet, and felt the whip of salt wind, and heard the ache of the ship's timber, always under assault; if she told of a desert, you were immediately parched and dessicated; did she speak of a garden, you were amid nodding and redolent vegetation; of hunger, you were pinched and starved, no matter how recent your corporeal meal in this world.

Indeed to try to catch her voice on paper is to miss most of the music of it in the air; and while I do not think I want for some small talent, I am not fool enough to think I have sufficient art to re-create it here; so I will simply report, as journalist, that she spoke of being at sea, for many weeks, crossing the "eastern ocean," as she said, which could mean any of many, but I took to be the Atlantic; how she slipped aboard a fishing boat, and then a tramp steamer, hiding in the wet darkness of the nether reaches, and stealing food when she could find it, which was seldom; terrified of being found out, and thrown overboard, or worse; being curled and huddled in the same position for hours and even days, and being so stiff and sore that she many times thought she would never move again, and end her young days a rigid corpse, to be gnawed by rats and reduced to gobbets of bone and buttons; twice catching and eating rats herself, driven to the extreme by hunger, and leaving nothing but their skulls and tails, which she could for some reason not stomach; enduring the savage roll and roil of a ship in storm, when the battering of the waves went on for days, and the very idea of the storm abating lost all possibility; the sort of shivering madness that comes from being sleepless, and wet, and ravenous, for weeks and weeks; her escape from the ship finally when it achieved port, in a city where she did not know the language, and walked between walls of snow higher than her head; her slow and complicated journey across a continent, city to city, village to farm, town to train, walking through a forest here, along a river there, stopping to cook or clean for someone, to work as a maid, to help with harvest, to serve beer and fend off the amorous intentions of men, and twice a woman; moving west without a destination in mind, but only an idea—something to do with the angle of light, and the smell of the sea, and houses made of wood and not stone; something to do with valleys of farms and crops, and waters filled with fish, and hills and mountains where there were more trees and animals than you could count in a lifetime. "A certain profligacy of creation," she said at one point, a phrase I never forgot. It wasn't that she ever expected to find a place where you didn't have to work to survive, where many people would be amicable, where the weather did not constantly measure your endurance, where the landscape conspired not to starve and winnow and frighten off its inhabitants but offer them such sustenance as they could find with suitable effort; she never dreamed of such a place, and whosoever does dream of that place is not suited for this world, which is both a gift and a trial, the latter somehow a condition of the former. But having arrived finally in San Francisco, by roads and paths too byzantine to recount, she had thought, one fine morning atop Blue

Mountain, in the very center of the city, *this is my place*; and so it had been ever since.

In point of fact, concluded Mrs Carson, as she bent to put two loaves of sourdough bread into the oven, she had found the rooming house on Bush Street that very same day, and soon came into possession of it (another complicated tale for another time, she said), and a wonderful place it had proven to be, as I now knew for myself; "and on that note I will conclude, Mr Stevenson," she said, "for dinner will be ready in eight minutes exactly, and if ever there was a dinner to eat steaming from the pan, it is fresh herring, so will you find Mr Carson, and bring him to the table, with my affectionate compliments?"

February 1, 1880, Oakland

Dearest Louis,

The briefest of notes to say we are all recovered here
at last, and await a visit Saturday by the estimable
R. L. Stevenson, of the Stevensons of Edinburgh, a young
author of whom much will be known in future, and the
world will ring with applause and approbation, for
centuries to come too, so that centuries from now, on any
one day in a hundred countries, you will find a reader
absorbed utterly in his books, and books of every kind!—
such books as were never written before, and never could
be imitated after, for the very dash and verve and wit of
the man himself was in them, shot through every sentence,
enlivening every page, so that his books glowed and

sizzled on the shelves, and had to be taken out regularly
and read for an hour, to calm their feverish energies!

Your most loving,
Fanny

The rooming house, I should say, was occupied by more than
the Carsons and myself; but the other residents were in the
main temporary, a few days or a week at a time, so that my
acquaintance with them was slim as a rule, although there
were a few with whom I conversed at some length, absorbed
by their stories and their manners of telling them; I think
now that the house on Bush Street was a sort of literary university to me in ways that my own university in Edinburgh
had not been, though the streets and lanes of that gray city
taught me much about human nature and its many characters
and flavors. But so did Bush Street, and as I was near thirty,
and about to be married and a sort of father, perhaps I was
much the better student of genuine story than I had been at
twenty, when I was mostly absorbed by flash and dash.

Most of the other brief residents were maritime men, who
came to Bush Street because of Mr John Carson, who appeared to know every sailor, chandler, dockman, boatswain,
and able-bodied seaman who had ever passed through the
city; it was wonderful to see him greet this one in Spanish
and that one in Russian, and to make gestures of goodwill
and companionship in the physical vocabularies of a dozen
nations, bowing low to the second mate from China and
hailing the man from Melbourne in the rough sunny language

of faraway Australia, a culture that seemed to use a flurry of fists as a genial how-do-you-do.

But it was not just seafolk who enlivened Mrs Carson's house; I remember two girls from Ireland who passed through, staying two and three weeks, respectively, until they found work as maids, the neither of them speaking a word during their residence except to Mrs Carson, and that in the melodious Gaelic; not even Mr Carson's bonhomie could elicit a syllable from them, though the Lord knows he tried; he was a man of the most friendly attentiveness, and he saw plain that they were terribly frightened and lonely. But they huddled near Mrs Carson like fawns behind their doe, until she saw them off to their new positions; and it tells you something of Mrs Carson that she walked them herself to their new houses, and had thorough discussions with the people there, before she would deign to leave; and in each case she returned twice a week to that address for a while, before she was assured that all was well and her chicks were safe.

I remember a man with a wooden leg, who said his name was Silver, and who told entrancing stories of the South Seas; and there were two men who claimed to be fallen royalty, swindled of their inheritances by devious means; there was an actor whose particular skill was performing famous oratorical passages, while dressed as that original person, so that his trunk was packed with the costumes of Cicero and Pericles and Demosthenes, who all appeared to have worn the same voluminous gown. There was a man who had been a bear hunter in the furthest reaches of Canada, where he swore there were blue bears, and white bears, and bears twice as tall as the tallest man; I remember him particularly because he looked rather like a bear himself, grizzled and furred all over, and wearing a claw from a bear he said he had personally fought several times, each time to a draw, and finally he and the bear had exchanged gifts as tokens of grudging respect, the bear surrendering a claw, and the man one of his rear teeth; and indeed he had a back tooth missing, as he was quite happy to show us.

It was one brief resident in particular, however, who led me to the next of Mr Carson's remarkable adventures, and it came about this way. One evening, as Mr Carson and I sat by the fire smoking after dinner, there came a knock on the door, and in came an older gentleman; it was a terribly wet night, as I recall, and Mrs Carson helped him unwrap his dripping coats, and brought him in to the blaze. For a moment the man stood facing the fire, soaking up the blessed heat, and I noticed his few wisps of hair, and a truly gargantuan beard. Then he turned to greet us politely; at which point Mr Carson leapt up out of his chair, flung away his cigar, and embraced the visitor like a beloved lost brother. I sat there agape at the suddenness and ferocity of his affections; and then I noticed that the other man was weeping silently, his face pressed into Mr Carson's shoulder almost like a child nestles into the shelter of his father.

A moment later the visitor had a brandy and a seat by the hearth, and sat hunched and silent as Mr Carson began to tell me something of who he was, and how they knew each other, and how they would be closer than brothers until they died, and afterward too, for some bonds cannot be severed by death.

"I could tell you about my friend here for days on end, and never come to the end of the brave things he has done, and the admirable humility with which he did them, and the many astounding things he has done since we first met," said Mr Carson slowly—he was, I could tell, choosing his way among the possible skeins of story, and picking carefully which to trace, and which to leave in shadow; it is a surpassing art, as I have learned, to know which things *not* to say or write, so that those that *do* see light are not obscured by tangles of lesser growth, so to speak.

"I could tell you of the path he chose as a young man," continued Mr Carson, "and the many young people he helped, and the fine teacher he became, so much so that there are a thousand men today who count him the best teacher they ever knew, the man who turned them from selfish and tumultuous ruffians to be men of character and grace; or I could tell you of what he became later, and is now, as famous in his line as any man in the country in another; but he would be the first to say that what he was, and what he is now by the measure of the world, is not what matters most to him in his life; and it is the day and night that matters most to him that I will tell you, for I was there with him, and I will never forget them either, and those awful hours are what made us brothers for life, and beyond, too.

"I have told you, Mr Stevenson, that I was here in San Francisco in 1864, as our war between the states still raged; but I did not tell you that I had been *in* the war, as a soldier, for two long years before that, on what we will call the blue side, the gray being our ostensible enemies, though they were from the same soil and water and air as us, and spoke the same tongue, and in every way were exactly like us. It is easy to say now that the two sides were motivated by a political divide so vast that we must needs shed blood to decide the matter, but I can tell you, and my dear friend here can absolutely attest, that this was not so, and we fought only to protect our friends and brothers from death and dismemberment. That is the only reason that men fight wars, Mr Stevenson, despite what is said about states' rights, and slavery, and the abrogation of treaties; you may take it from me that every history book is filled with lies, and not one man in ten thousand ever ponders which prince ought to have the throne, or which river ought to be the national boundary, or which side shall have the coveted farmland, and which the exhausted fields of nettle; no, all we think about, as we charge at each other with weapons at the ready, is that *those* men would do harm to *my* friends, and they must be stopped from doing so, if necessary at the price of my brief life. It is easiest to think that they are not *men* at all who would murder your companions, but the crudest of animals, not worth the price of a lamb, and better off exterminated; and this is how most wars are fought, but not ours, for in our war both sides knew the other to be at least our own countrymen, if not, in many cases, actual neighbors and relations, classmates and boys met once on fields of play.

"I tell you all this so you will understand the intensity of what happened that day. It was the height of summer—a warm and humid morning, and then hotter and dustier as the day went on, and we men in blue wearing wool; I remember a sudden ferocious thunderstorm late in the afternoon, washing over the devastation like another Flood.

"We were to attack across a wheat field. There were some five hundred of us, I suppose, and we had no notion of our opposing numbers, or their position; we were told only to attack, and overwhelm the gray line, and advance into the fringe of trees, as far as we could safely defend thereafter. We could see the flickering leaves of the trees across the field—red oaks and white oaks, with here and there copses of hickory and ash, and a huge old black cherry tree. Odd that I would remember the trees so well, but I do, and I can see them yet— burly old oaks with arms like muscles, and the young vibrant trees leaping up where they could find a hint of light. What is more beautiful than a summer forest, especially in this green and blessed land, where creeks and streams wander everywhere, and the air is sown with innumerable birds?

"The birds—perhaps that should have been a sign for us, that the birds were silent or absent, but we did not read it, because we were exhausted, and filled with trepidation, and weary beyond words after two days of furious battles, during which most of our friends had been slain or horribly wounded. I remember that we sprawled at the edge of the field, resting as best we could before the assault; and there was a curious haunted feeling among us, as if each knew we would not see another day, but be killed almost to a man; and that battle was one where it would be better to die, than to live on without your legs, or arms, or the bottom half of your face—better to die quickly than to wake up screaming in the surgeon's tent, and know that the rest of your days would be red searing pain, and all you could reasonably hope for in life was a chance to end it, a chance to finish for yourself what bullets and shells had begun.

"My friend here sensed our mood, and indeed shared it, as he had shared everything else with us. He was a chaplain—*the* chaplain, *our* chaplain, and he had been nearly three years in the brigade, arriving as it formed in New York, and marching with it through all the savagery from the start—Yorktown, Fair Oaks, Antietam, Fredericksburg, and now Gettysburg. He knew us, he *was* us, and not once that any of us ever knew did he shirk from what he saw as his duty, to minister to the men in every way—he nursed the sick, and bound the wounded, and carried men when they could not walk, and heard their confessions, and blessed them as they died. I saw for myself more times than I could count how he went fearless into the line of fire to salve a man's pain, or bring him back to safety; and for that quiet calm tireless bravery we loved him, and admired him, and while there were those among us who thought him mad, and his religion a barbaric cult, even so not one among us failed to

71

salute the courage and character of the man himself, beneath the vestments of the priest.

"So that morning when he arose to speak, he had our every ear, weary and frightened though we were. He climbed up on a boulder, and wrapped a purple cloth around his neck, and raised his hands, and said that through the power vested in him by his god, he cleansed us of our sins. And he said firmly that to kill the men in gray today was no sin at all, but our bound duty, and that duty we must do with all our might and main, and the man who wavered and hesitated would be struck down instantly by the angel of death, and his bones would lie unburied and unblessed, and his soul consigned to the flames until the end of time.

"I had never seen him in this sort of mood, and while his voice rang and he seemed exalted, it did seem unlike him, to be pronouncing fates so sternly, and to be urging death, when he had for so long been such an agent of mercy; but some strange fit was upon him, and when he was finished there was a roar from the men, and we plunged into the wheat field to attack the gray line.

"I remember the deep scent of the black soil there, rich and thick and dense and redolent of life and crops and produce; I remember the wind swaying the stalks of wheat, as if a huge hand was idly brushing the earth's pelt; I remember that lovely line of ash and oak, with the big black cherry tree like a chieftain in their midst; I remember the gasping and clanking and cursing as we sprinted toward those trees; and then I remember the roar of murderous fire that cut us down like a scythe slices wheat. They had been waiting for us; there were three times as many of them as us, and they shot us to pieces, shot us to death, shot us down so fast and so completely that by the time their shooting subsided, a few minutes later, our brigade was a thing of the past, our name only a memory, the few survivors sent to other regiments, the wheat field so draped with bodies that plows will uncover bullets and buttons for a century to come.

"I was hit, high in the shoulder, and down I went, and that was all I knew until I awoke in the night; I remember staring at the stars for what seemed like a long time until my senses flooded back and I knew them to be stars, and myself nearly a corpse. I managed then to crawl back to our side of the field; I was unsure which *was* our side until I came upon the very boulder on which my friend had issued his speech, and there, to my amazement, I found the very man, huddled and still. I thought he was dead, until he stirred, and then I thought he had been driven mad, because all he could do for a while was gibber and mew, and scratch at his face with his fingernails like a lunatic.

"How long we sat there by the rock I do not know—much of the night, I suppose. I remember the awful silence, relieved only by the occasional scream or moan or whimper from the field. Twice I heard voices among the oak trees— our men or theirs, I never did discover. No wind, no moon, no other survivors that I knew, no officers, no soldiers retrieving the dead or retrieving the wounded; no horses rustling, no campfires, nothing. It was as if we had passed into another world from the one we were in during the day, and everything we knew was gone or ghostly. More than once that night I did conclude that I was dead, and this was the afterworld, to which my friend had also been assigned for mysterious reasons.

"Finally he seemed to recover something of his wits, and he started to murmur broken and halting words: '*I did this*,' he said. 'I sent them to their deaths. I murdered them with my own mouth. My words were the very bullets. Who am I to speak of sin, who has murdered so many men? Who am I? My boys, my brothers, my beloved brothers . . . ,' and so on in this vein, all the while scratching madly at his face until the blood poured down into his coat—and soaking his purple cloth too, the very one he had worn while giving his speech, though now it was torn and stained.

"I have told you stories, sir, of my time in Sarawak, and on the island of the eagles, and it will be a pleasure and an honor to tell you many more stories of the things that happened to me in various quarters of the world, in the wettest wildernesses and the hottest dry deserts, in this ship and that, in moments of tumult and moments of surpassing serenity; but the one story I cannot find proper words for is the story of the rest of that night, and our next few days. To sketch it in the roughest terms I would say that we walked out of the war, and into the rest of our lives—walking away not from cowardice, or fear, or even horror at the slaughter we had seen and endured, the horror that had taken most of our friends and companions, but because in some way we were dead, too—evanesced, vanished, finished, plucked from this life into some other state—I suppose now a sort of coma, or waking dream. We were no longer the men we had been before the battle. Like our companions who ran into the stubble and never returned, nor did we return, but were taken up somehow, and our feet set upon the dark road, and we knew not our destination or direction.

"It is vague to me now, what we did; we staggered north and east, along streambeds and through forests, walking at night and sleeping in thickets during the day. I believe that we followed the moon, as I have a dim recollection of plodding along the path it drew for us. We held hands sometimes, like small children; sometimes I carried my friend awhile; once he carried me, along the shore of a lake; I remember his feet dragging and shuffling in the shallow water, and the murmur of owls in the forest."

I stole a glance at the bearded man, Mr Carson's friend, and found him sitting hunched forward in his chair, his face in his hands, the firelight playing over his sparse gray hairs; as I watched Mr Carson reached over and most tenderly put his hand on his friend's shoulder, and his friend reached up instantly and gripped Mr Carson's hand with all his might.

"There is not much else to tell," said Mr Carson quietly. "It seems to me that we walked a very long time, and then finally found refuge with a pastor in a small mill town; he recognized my friend as a fellow priest, and betook himself to care for us, and give us shelter. I can see his face yet, but have lost his name; I believe he may have been a student at the college where my friend worked before he entered the war. A silent man most of the time, and terse when he was not silent, but for all that a gentle soul, who asked us no questions, but let us slowly come back to life in his rectory—my shoulder healing, my friend's mind returning.

"My friend says that what he remembers of that time is certain angles of light, like messages or mysterious letters, and the music of rivers and creeks and streams, to which he became much attached, and along which he spent most of his time, as he recovered his balance over some weeks; but what I remember is a night when the pastor asked us to come with him to confront a farmer who was, the pastor told us, essentially enslaving a foreign servant. He did not share any more detail, but asked us to provide our military bearing and physical 'substance,' as he said, while he endeavored to make things right. This we did, of course, and not only in gratitude to the pastor but with an honest interest in freeing an innocent captive; what else, as my friend here said, was the war *for*, if not to murder the system by which one man sells and buys another, or purchases girls for his amusement?

"That evening's odd work by itself would be a story for a week by the fire, but suffice it to say that the pastor did persuade the farmer to relinquish his hold on the girl, with some disputation on the farmer's part overcome by sensible calculation of forces for and against his point of view. My friend and I waited on the porch, as the pastor helped the young lady prepare her exit; the farmer had agreed to provide a horse and carriage to expiate his debt; it turned out he had never paid the girl a cent in the long months she had worked there as a kitchen maid, with constant assaults upon her dignity, and abuse heaped upon her for the slightest error, though she had never been a maid, and did not speak our language, and there was no wife or additional servant to instruct her in the ways and whims of the house; in effect she was entrapped and imprisoned, with no appeal or chance of redress, until the pastor had realized her straits.

"That was another moonlit night, as I remember; the carriage was to head straight down a lane washed by the light, and all that awaited was the girl herself, gathering the last of her scarce possessions. Finally out came the pastor, walking with her, and helping her up into the carriage; my friend and I were on the porch, keeping an eye on the angry farmer. The pastor stepped back from the carriage, and the girl made ready to go, but just then, for some reason—perhaps curiosity about the men who had helped to free her—she turned and looked at us. It was only for a second or two, and then away she clattered down the road; but in that instant I saw the face of the girl in the stone village!"

And just then, as if mentioning that face had been a clarion call, Mrs Carson appeared, with black coffees for each of us, and a bowl of steaming oyster soup for the bearded man: "It will restore you better than any medicine could, as you will remember from the last time," she said, and he stood and bowed and kissed her hand, a gesture I had rarely seen in America, and rather missed, as a sign, from man to woman, of courtly respect, or reverence.

So the moment was broken, and the story suspended, and the time to retire soon upon us. Mr and Mrs Carson said goodnight, and as I prepared to go upstairs I asked the gentleman his plans—a few days enjoying the city, or exploring the wild mountains and pastoral valleys? No, no, he said; he was in the city just for tonight, and had come specifically to see Mr and Mrs Carson, who were something like medicine to him, restorative, *resurrective,* in the language of his theology; he could not go a year without their presence in his life, even in the briefest dose, like now, for reasons he did not wholly understand. He supposed, he said, that if you tried to explain it sensibly, you could say that he saved my life, and she is, as you see for yourself, a pure clear energy of rare quality, so exposure to my savior, and to a soul as genuine and refreshing as Mrs Carson, is of course a happy jolt; but there is more to it than that, much more. It has something to do with restoration and resurrection; that is as close as I can come to articulating it. I need to see them and hear them and have them physically about me sometimes; I need to drink them in, to hear their voices, to feel their hands on my shoulder. I fear that there will come a time when they are dead and I am not; and should that sadness ever come to pass, I know that I too will soon be dead, for I believe that if they are not in this world, soon enough neither will I be; but I *do* have faith, I *do* believe with all my heart, I *know,* as man and priest, that I will be reunited with them in the world to come; and that conviction is sometimes the one thing that sees me through the dark nights that we all face—priests perhaps above all other men.

And in the morning he was gone, "back to his beloved college in the faraway fields," said Mr Carson with a smile; and Mrs Carson, to honor and celebrate his brief visit, made the most appetizing bubbling oyster stew that night, and Mr Carson found bottles of dusty old Beaujolais, and we had a wonderful dinner, augmented by several maritime friends of Mr Carson's, briefly in the city and visiting their old ship-mate before heading back into the Pacific; I well remember those men around the table murmuring the names of their past and future ports of call, even the names so alluring and redolent and whispering of sunlight and sheets of sudden rain and remote beauty almost beyond the reach of words to describe it: Papeete, Moorea, Manihiki, Raiatea, Huahine, Rarotonga, Upolu . . .

5

THOUGH I HAD BUT PENNIES IN MY POCKET at that time, still, I was curiously rich in time to spend as I saw fit, for while I tried to work ten or twelve hours a day at my desk, eventually my imagination would falter and wane, and I would have to stand up and move about, and even, occasionally, blessedly, eat; I knew myself well enough as a writer by then to know that anything written in exhaustion would be prim and wan and dessicated, and not worth the ink on the page. Even then, while still in my twenties, I was dimly aware that there was one sort of writing that discusses and comments and informs, at best usefully, and sometimes quite beautifully; but there is also another sort of writing altogether, that uses every conceivable tool and angle and approach and trick and sleight-of-hand to reach for that which is deep and inarticulate in each one of us; and it was on Bush Street that I first began to perceive that I might be capable of this latter thing.

I had loved the essay, for it is the form closest to the human voice, closest to the general loose and free and untrammeled manner of human thought; but for the most part, when I was young, I did but add to the mountain of mannered essays, poor writings all too conscious of themselves in their delivery, like actors who are trying too hard to act, rather than simply *being* the character portrayed. But on Bush Street I began to sense that the deeper essay was possible, one that sought, in a real sense, to approach that for which we do not have good words, or words at all; and too I began to see how a fiction could hint at a deeper truth than any essay or article could achieve, though the latter reveled in their veracity, and dismissed novels as only airy wisps and dreams. As I finished the one small novel I had begun in Monterey, then, I began to dimly dream others—novels where I could, at one level, tell a roaring tale of adventure and skullduggery, but at other levels perhaps hint or suggest things we know about ourselves and our lives but do not often, if at all, bring up into the light to examine: our deep inarticulate love for our friends; the ways that we are both dark and light in our hearts, and ever the two sides struggle for mastery; the prickly tool and virtue and sin, all at once, that pride is, in both man and woman; the manner in which a man can be a rogue and a conspirator, and yet be brave and kindly in surprising ways; the way nationality and character can be both glory and prison; the way religions can be wonderful keel on which to build the ship of a soul, and the easy excuse for the most horrid murders; the way the expectations of a father—in a way, the very fabric of his love and hope for his child, exposed for all to see—can be a veritable jail for his offspring, or the wind that blows the young as far from the old as it is possible to go.

All these things and more I began to believe could be stitched in and among and below other layers and levels of story; and there are times now when I wonder if my teacher in this matter was not Mr Carson, for not only were his stories headlong and wonderful, but I began to hear, like a faint music, some other stories being told, or hinted at, beneath the rush of surface events. It struck me one day, for example, that he had never hesitated to pursue the boy Adil through the jungles of Sarawak, though any number of other men might have given up the boy as lost, or calculated that the danger in his recovery outweighed the call of duty or friendship, or casually turned away, concluding that one less brown boy in a world crammed with them was no particular loss. Similarly there by the rock, at the edge of the wheat field through which so many men rushed to their deaths, Mr Carson did not hesitate to escort his friend the priest away not only from the battlefield but right out of the war itself; and I realized that I had not asked him how it was that he and his companion walked clean out of the Union Army, though the War Between the States did not end until two years later. So it was that I began to marvel not just at Mr Carson's tumultuous adventures, but at the man himself, and at the subtle currents of his heart; and I began to wonder if he was not very consciously and deliberately choosing particular chapters of his life to tell, in order to tell me other things, perhaps—about the nature and power of stories, about how decisions not only reflect but create character, about how stories actually shape our lives; could it be that the words we choose to have resident in our mouths act as a sort of mysterious food, and soak down into our blood and bones, and form that which we wish to be? We think this to be so, do we not?, insofar as lewd and vulgar language, and look upon those who berate and blaspheme as avatars and exemplars of the foulness they emit, just as volcanoes are made of the lava they vomit forth into the innocent air.

I put these questions to him that evening by the fire, and he smiled, and contemplated his cigar for a moment, and then he said, "You will remember that I left you, as it were, on the porch of the farmer's house, in a little mill town that my friend knew well; I will tell you that this house was in Michigan, but I cannot tell you where; but what happened to me after that night is a long story and I believe Mrs Carson will call us to dinner in only twenty minutes. I would be a poor storyteller indeed did I compress such an odyssey into so small a time. Suffice it to whet your appetite when I say that from there to here entailed a train, a riverboat, a riveting man named Tondzaosha, some weeks spent in the forests and inlets of western Canada, and finally a stroke of luck that still gives me pause, and makes me wonder if indeed there *is* a force far beyond our grasp that arranges the affairs of men, or at the least presents them with possibilities, some of which lead to joy far deeper than any I had ever imagined possible.

"So let me save that story for another time. But I will give you the beginnings of another, if you wish; for I have been thinking tonight of a young man I met in Australia, just last year, on the quays of Sydney Harbor, the most beautiful harbor in the world, as we both agreed, and both of us men of the sea, with some thorough experience in bays and anchorages and winds and weathers.

"The last day of January this was, which is the height of summer there, on the other side of the world; and I was between ships, having left one and not yet found another; and in the ancient way of mariners I went down to the docks, just as you do sometimes here, for reasons you cannot name—myself, I think there is a yearning in every man for the sea, perhaps because it is the mother of all things, the place from whence emerged first life, says my friend Mr Wallace; and if Mr Wallace says a thing, you may take it as being so.

"You are an author, Mr Stevenson, and I am only a sailor, but not even you, I think, could find words for the beauty of a high summer day in that loveliest of cities, that driest and strangest of countries. The clarity of the sun, seemingly coming from a different angle than we are used to here on the top half of the world; the bright red parrots and the tremendous fruit bats, as big as herons; the immense gum and eucalyptus trees, which shed their bark but keep their leaves; the harbor itself, with so many bays and inlets and secret corners that you could spend a lifetime exploring its reaches, and hardly see the same scene twice . . . well, Mr Stevenson, I will tell you I see it in my dreams yet, and someday I will return, this time with Mrs Carson, to see what we shall see, and to visit a few people I count among my dearest friends.

"There I sat on the quay, Mr Stevenson, a man without a care or a worry, for I had been paid off by my ship, and had no fear of finding another berth—there were ships almost beyond counting in the harbor, and every third one of them I could see loose or tied would touch eventually in San Francisco, and need an experienced hand for the journey— sometimes I think all ships under all flags eventually visit San Francisco, which perhaps exerts a magnetic pull on all the craft of the world, and calls to each to visit occasionally, as you would bend your own journey, given half the chance, to see a beloved aunt or grandparent.

"There sat I, as I said, basking in the morning sun, idly contemplating fish and beer for lunch, when right up before me slides a lovely clipper ship to berth: the *Duke of Sutherland,* a thousand tons, from London, carrying who knows what, but very probably here for wool, to carry back to England for high and healthy profit.

"I watched it berth with real interest, for there are few things in life more beautiful than a clipper ship, all lean lines and set to race before the wind, and this one was well handled, so it was a workingman's pleasure to see it maneuvered with easy skill into its resting place, and the cargo unloaded smoothly and swiftly. Then I watched its crew be released, half and half in the traditional way, for shore leave; and last to depart among this first contingent was a thin young fellow with one of those earnest halfhearted beards men grow at age twenty or so—the youth fully intent on having a beard, and the beard not yet convinced that it is ready for its debut.

"Up he came to me, where I sat on a bench above the quay, and he greeted me politely—a strong accent, east of Germany but west of Russia, as I read it—and asked if he might sit with me a few moments, to get his land bearings, and converse in English, for he was set on fluency in that tongue, and had read Shakespeare on the voyage out from London. Something there was intent and arresting about the fellow—he was hungry to ask or tell me something—and I bid him sit and unburden his mind.

"We were on that bench above the harbor for hours, he and I, and I will always remember those hours, I think. For one, there was the glorious panoply of the harbor and its armada of cargo and passenger ships from around the world spread before us—'one of the finest, most beautiful, vast, and safe bays the sun ever shone upon,' as the young man said, and right he was. Behind and around us the golden glowing city—George Street, where sailors liked to go to eat, and the old King's Head pub on the hill, a favorite of seagoing cooks and stewards and boatswains, for reasons no one knew. The great lush gardens, the brawling streets, the bronze stone churches and houses built, so it was said, by the poor convicts transported by the heartless empire to the far edge of the world, there to slave under a strange sun, watched by the unseen natives, who must have many times wondered what manner of men were these, to enslave their

own people, and so often for the theft of a loaf of bread, a muttered insult to the rich man, the poaching of a hen when the children were starving.

"But more riveting than the glittering scene before us was the young man's talk, for he poured out his heart, and laid out not only his past but the future he could only dimly see yet greatly craved; and more than that, something in him was deeply wise, despite his youth, and his own tumultuous emotions, the latter of which had already almost unmoored him. He had, he confessed, nearly done away with himself at one point, in despair at obstacles at every turn, and only stopped his hand when he realized that he could never then unspool all the stories he felt rising in him—'stories that *must* be told, Mr Carson, *must* be written down, or they will evanesce, and be imprisoned for another thousand years, awaiting another teller—for stories are themselves deathless, and for every one told, a hundred thousand jostle for a tongue to tell them also—but so many never emerge on paper or by a fire at night, and back they must go into the shadows; you can sense them sometimes, rustling just out of earshot—don't you sense them, Mr Carson? Don't you?'

"This was how he talked, mysterious and piercing, so that one moment you thought him slightly mad, and the next a sort of elegant mystic. He had a way of staring at you as he spoke, so that somehow you felt you and he had been friends for many years, though we were acquaintances only of an hour; and too, when he was silent he was a youth, and when he spoke he was a man of vast experience and long contemplation.

"He told me of his childhood in Poland, and of the time he and his parents were exiled into the remote Russian north, cold gray months he never forgot; he said he still awoke sometimes at sea, especially in storms, believing he was again imprisoned on the taiga, watching his parents cough themselves to death. He told me of being orphaned at age eleven, and of going to sea for the first time at age sixteen, first with coasters from Marseilles, and then finally with English ships. He loved life at sea, he said, loved everything about it, even the arduous work and the weeks of wet clothing, for 'on the ship, on the sea,' he said, 'you are plunged into the stories, the stories are everywhere about you, waiting so anxiously; I ask the men, and they tell me every story they know, liking me for listening so attentively, and when we land, away I go into the docks and streets and lanes, and there are more stories waiting for me than there are pebbles in the road; and stories in lands other than your own, you know, are delighted to see a stranger, for he will be interested in the stories that the natives think common and shallow, and no longer tell, or hear; it is as if their ears are stopped, but mine, having never been touched by words in that place, are a fresh harbor; never have I heard so many stories as I have in foreign ports. I could write a hundred books of the stories I have been told on and around the sea, and that is what I mean to do, Mr Carson, when my voyages are finished at last.'

"He had a plan, you see; he was intent on it, and he knew

the end of the first part of his life and the advent of the second almost to the day, it seemed. 'Ten more years, Mr Carson, perhaps fifteen, for I wish to rise from seaman to mate to master, and command sailing ships from one end of the compass to the other, and then begin to write my books, and never stop doing so, until I am dead, and can be returned to the mud, to be of use only in driving flowers upward in the spring. The stories must out, you see; and if I am granted time and energy, out they will come, a whole shelf of them, and at least I will have saved a hundred or a thousand from the darkness. And I will have sailed the whole blue wilderness of the world, too, a great thing.'

"It wasn't all him, of course, over those hours; he had a wonderful capacity for alert silence, a sort of active hunger for what you would say next, so that you felt, once embarked on a story, that it was almost being pulled from you bodily by his nervous energy; this was not a man with whom you could wander off on tangents, and shuffle here and there in the forest of a tale; no, with him you must tell it straight, as deeply and honestly as you can, leaving nothing out but neither straying off the main path, until you came to the end.

"It took me a while to realize that what he listened most assiduously for was not action, or plot, but emotion and character; what *happened* was less interesting to him than *why* it happened, and that in turn was less interesting than *who*; his whole orientation was personality and character, who people really were under their intricate masks and disguises, appurtenances and appearances, habits and excuses. I think now

91

that what fascinated him was how people conducted themselves in a world he thought was without pity and direction, set in motion and then abandoned to its own devices; and I think too that what fascinated him most deeply was how people managed their lives, knowing that all the things we use as compasses and safeguards are less substantial than shadows. He did not believe in gods, governments, moral laws, or any rules in the universe other than the undeniable physics that spins the earth around the sun and sends starlight toward us through uncountable time; so that his whole interest in life was how we manage to go on, what ephemera and ritual we construct as support, what poses we assume with others of our kind, and how true we are to that which we hope ourselves to be.

"It was not all him speaking, as I said, and over the course of our time on the bench I believe he heard every voyage I had ever had, every adventure, every expedition, every journey; he soaked up every detail of my ships and sailing, and he knew every obscure part of our mutual profession, too, I must say; and when finally the time came for him to join his crewmates at dinner, and for me to be about looking for my next berth, I had come to believe that here before me, young as he was, was a great man in the making. Someday the world will sing the praises of that young man, I am convinced; in quite the same way, Mr Stevenson, as songs may well be sung of you; who is to say what is possible and what is not, when so much of who we are is invisible and yet to come? Are we not like ships, as my young Polish friend said, with so much unseen beneath the waterline, and so much of that unseen material densely packed and intricately built, and crammed with stories and dreams? So to look at a man's face and clothing and boots, or to ask after his nativity and parentage and occupation, and draw from those small clues any substantive knowledge of his ambition and will, his character and possibility, the revolution and grace of his mind, his destination and fate, is a foolish mistake, albeit one made all day every day by most of the world.

"We finally rose from our remarkable bench, him to dine with his mates, and me to set about finding a ship, and we shook hands for a long while with real affection, and something like reverence; I think both of us were startled and moved to have found something like a brother, here at the other end of the world; and, too, there is a deep feeling in all of us, I think, when we feel we have been thoroughly and carefully *listened* to, by a perceptive soul; this is the brilliance of the idea of religious confession, is it not, that a burden is eased simply by being conveyed in words to another set of willing shoulders, or ears? And of course very often when we carefully explain ourselves to another, we hear something in ourselves that had been hidden. *Quod locutus est verus*—that which is spoken is real.

"Something like that must have happened in me, for as we turned to go, he turned back, and took me by the arm—he had a grip like a wrestler, for all that he was a slight youth—and he said that I must find the girl now; that no more time could be allowed to pass before I bent every iota of my energy in the search. I was startled, I can tell you, for I had not realized I had so unburdened my heart about the girl on Sliabh Mór, but *he* had heard, and heard too not just what I said, but what I had left unsaid, even to myself.

"'I cannot guess at what will happen when you *do* find her,' he said, 'although I can say with confidence that you *will*; and lest you think I am inserting myself into your private affairs, allow me to say that I am only articulating what you have said to me today with all your heart and mind and soul. That girl's face glows behind every word you said to me; and I think you know this, and you know what you must do, and perhaps you have only been waiting until someone issued you an order to set sail upon that journey. I am only a seaman today, Mr Carson, a mere able-body at the bottom of the manifest; but I *will* command a ship someday, and I will issue my first order today, to a man I will always think of henceforth as a friend. Go and get you a ship, and find that girl from the empty stone village, and then who knows what will happen? Not God, for there is no such thing, much as we yearn and dream; but something better, perhaps; something for which no writer has yet found the suitable word.'

"And away he went up the hill toward The Rocks, where sailors have congregated since the first ships found the vast continent of the antipodes. I stood there a long while, transfixed, and then, Mr Stevenson, I set about the last of my adventures in several quarters of the world; but who is this waving us to dinner but the estimable Mrs Carson herself, and I believe that the alluring smell slipping out from behind her is oysters baked and broiled. I would walk many miles for oysters baked and broiled, Mr Stevenson, many miles; and if you are wise, you will walk these few feet to the kitchen with me, and we shall fall upon the luckless bivalves, and annihilate them utterly, and count ourselves the luckiest men in the world tonight, for these oysters have passed through Mrs Carson's hands on the way to the table, and that passage makes all the difference between mere eating and fine dining. Also we will have excellent wine, and our companion at table will be Mrs Carson, and you can take it from me that there is no table companion quite as excellent as Mrs Carson—but you know for yourself now, I am sure. . . ."

February 6, 1880, Bush Street, San Francisco

My dear Colvin,

I write this letter first to thank you for so assiduously and energetically shopping my inky creations in the streets of dirty old London; you are in no uncertain terms keeping body and soul together, not only for the scarecrowish undersigned but in large part for Fanny and the children—*her* children, I should say, editor-careful, though I hope with all my heart that someday they will say that they are in some way mine also—I do hope to be a decent stepfather, though there is not much of me, and what rags and bones there are always a-wrack with cough. Still, if I but continue to exist corporeally, and show up at table with them every day, and make the slightest effort on their behalf, I will be ten times the father they had before—the original paternal issue, though according to Fanny he issued right out the door as soon as the children were born.

But I cannot lambaste the lieutenant, for it is he who

must give Fanny the deed to the cottage in Oakland, or she will have not a farthing with which to feed and house her chicks—our plan is to marry the instant she owns the document, and is a woman of property and means, and then sell the house instanter, and embark on the briefest of honeymoons in the vineyards north of the city. After that I do not know; we talk of summer in Scotland, so that she can meet my mother and father, and you, and so many other dear friends. A careful man would lay his plans like railroad ties along the path ahead, but I cannot see that far, and cannot afford the timbers; I hoist only my trusty pen all day, and write as fast and fiercely as I can, and haunt the post office, where they know me too well as the Author from Scotland who so desperately wishes for mail from his friends, reporting on another sale to another magazine— news like that, when it comes, sends me capering up Bush Street like a minstrel, singing and roistering as once I did in the lanes and alleys of Auld Reekie, when I was a university man in the Athens of the North.

So long ago those days seem to me, Colvin, so very far behind me, though that was but ten years ago; it seems incomprehensible that *I* was a roaring boy with a tankard in one hand and a maid in the other, a scandal and a scoundrel, a rascal and an abject lesson; but I knew myself even then it was merely a performance, a shout against what my father and family wished me to be—engineer, lawyer, pillar of Presbyterianism, sober stalwart of Edinburgh society. The problem, though, was that I knew quite clearly what I was not, and could never be, but did not know at all what I *was,* and could be; but I know that now, and *I have set my face like flint,* as old Isaiah sayeth, *and I shall not be confounded, and I shall not be ashamed.*

But I am a-wander in memory and the King James here, Colvin my dear, and I return posthaste to reporting my life on Bush Street, where I live like a sailor on the sea, working all the day from dawn to dusk, and sleeping four hours of every sixteen, and eating ravenously whatever appears in front of me from the ship's cook— although here I must tell you that never was there such a cook in the history of the world, and it will be a miracle if ever another cook ariseth to compare to her. It is my landlady of whom I speak, the estimable and incomparable Mrs Carson, and while a thousand songs might be sung of her culinary gifts, and rightfully and heartily they would be sung too, it is the soul of the woman that has a genius even greater than her way with viand and victual. For all my way with words, here I will stammer and stutter when I try to describe her fairly. Beautiful? Yes, but that is the last thing you would notice in her, though the first thing you would notice in another. Graceful? Yes—but again her grace is part and parcel of her being, and her physical grace is only an expression of a deeper thing that need express itself in this world somehow; you know what I mean, that the deepest things must find vessels in order to assume shape and enter this world; otherwise they would float and wander

too freely, and always be hint and suggestion and
intuition, rather than something we see and hear and
touch, to our amazement. So very many things there are
like this; and sometimes I think the deepest of all pleasures
is encountering them, and sensing and recognizing them,
and standing there awed and delighted, grateful that you
were given the eyes to see and the ears to hear.

My own ears are well used these days also, in the
evenings, as I with great pleasure and mounting
amazement pry an endless series of stories from Mrs
Carson's husband John, who has been all over the world
in various ships, and has had adventures of every
conceivable sort, in dense jungles and remote islands and
terrible battlefields, and, he says, in blazing deserts and
dripping forests and under the sea, though he has not told
me those stories whole as yet; but there is time, I daresay,
for I cannot imagine Fanny will come into possession of
the cottage until March at the earliest, and until that
moment we must continue our odd existence, me working
as hard as I possibly can to get money on which to
support my prospective family, and Fanny taking the
ferry over from Oakland once a week, so that we can kiss
on the dock, and share a sparse meal, and then back she
goes on the ferry, with me yearning as the boat steams
away, for she must be home to her boy, who is only
eleven years old; as he has no father, he cannot bear to
have no mother even for a night. I can understand him,
for I was that same boy at his age, and the night was filled

with spirits and terrors; I sometimes wonder if that sort of fervid imagination as a child fed the Author from Scotland, and created him, and feeds him still; for there are times when I am writing my stories now that the people and hills and swords and horses and dark tides in them are so real and vivid to me that I am startled back into this world when the candle gutters, and I look up and see the swirling mist of the city below, and hear the sorrowful moans of ships in the bay, and remember that I am here at the edge of America. And here I should conclude this bumbling letter, for even I, the most energetic of children, must sleep a few hours here and there, or else fall headlong into one of my own stories and never return—"all that was found of the missing Scotsman was his tattered coat, his trusty cigarettes, and the wedding ring he was to have slipped onto the finger of a lady in Oakland, who much mourns his disappearance."

> *Ever your most affectionate and*
> *grateful friend,*
> *R.L.S.*

I have not been as assiduous as I should be in reporting the actual scents and sounds and sensory verve of the great city in which I found myself that year; for San Francisco in 1880 was a wild world unto itself, unlike any city I had ever known.

My native Edinburgh, cold and wet and windy and swirling with snow, resonant with bells, wracked by prim greed and cold opinion, crowned by its ancient castle, lapped by green fields and hills, was surely and relentlessly Scottish, but it was also a great city of Europe, peer to Oslo and Brussels, cousin to London and Berlin and Moscow; for all its Caledonian character, Edinburgh is of a piece with the other stern grand cities of the continent, from Dublin to Prague, the old capitals of worn stone and soldiers' boots, of dark slums and inbred gentry; as were the other cities in which I had spent some time, from London to Paris to Zurich. Each was its own densely woven tale, of course, constructed over centuries or millennia by war and money and love and loss; but even in the sunniest cities of Europe there was the faint scent of ancient blood, and grim walls of stone that kept kings from slaves, and the smirk of churchmen long allied with the nobles who paid them to beseech heaven on their behalf.

But I found little of this in San Francisco. Yes, there were bastions of power, streets of old and new money, and forts where one could hear the rattle of weapons and the tramp of sergeants; but the true lifeblood of the city was its triple waterfront, from which came and went ships of every description from every part and corner of the world, and it seemed to me that the maritime nature of the city, thrust like a thumb into the eye of the sea, defined and dictated its character. Certainly it dictated its weather, so often mist and fog, and sheeting tides of rain, and a wind so steady you could steer by it in the street, blown due east in the morning and true west again at night; I always half-expected to see residents erect small personal sails, and whirl their way to work or school, tacking here and there as necessary with rigging made of string.

But the sea-soaked nature of the city also meant, it seems to me, that its residents were always facing great waters, and great waters are forces bigger than we are, for all we seek to control and channel them; so that there was perhaps less arrogance and braggadocio in San Francisco than in some other cities, less of the urge to dominate and enslave anything and everything, to create empires, to bring all things to heel. This is not to say there was any lack of greed and violence, which were as common tongues there as anywhere else; but if we can speak of the residents of a city as a whole, and say something true of many thousands of souls at once—a dangerous enterprise—I would say that San Franciscans then were busier with travel and transaction than with avid acquisition. They were constantly in motion, always about to leave, or just arrived home; and even the latter were already contemplating their next voyage, so that no sooner did you meet a friend in the street, and hear of his adventures in Alaska or Albuquerque, but he was away again, this time to Vladivostok, or Veracruz.

It was a city of soaring dreams, in one way, and of peaceful dreams, in another. It seemed to me that it was a launching-spot for a tremendous number of souls headed west and south and north, though never east; if ever there was a city facing in one direction and wholly uninterested in another, it was San Francisco then; in the four months I lived there I heard only two references to anything east of Oakland, and both those remarks were awed stories of the Sierra Nevada, the tremendous snowy mountains that rose along the border of California like the ramparts of heaven.

Yet the city was also a final refuge for many who had roamed the world, and finally found the home of their hearts; Mr and Mrs Carson, I thought, were two of these, and I met many more, in my time. And while I heard every sort of prosaic answer when I asked those people what brought and kept them here, each somehow also hinted at a deeper reason, having something to do with freedom from expectations, freedom from the past, often freedom from their families; we do not admit much that families can be a kind of prison from which we yearn to escape, yet this is incontrovertibly so, as I know too well myself.

Sometimes I would sit atop one of the city's many hills, and stare out at the sea to the west, and the immense bay to the east, and the wild seethe of inlet between them, and consider that here was a city shaped like the dreams of its residents, so many of whom wanted to be here at the end of the earth, the edge of the continent, the final mile of their voluminous country; here those who wished to live at the edge of all things did so, on a craggy peninsula that was both remote and the destination of ships and souls and stories from all over the world; another thing to love about San Francisco was that there were a hundred languages in its streets and lanes, and a man could easily walk in and out of a dozen tongues as he walked from one dock to another; being greeted here in Mandarin, and there in Mexican, and around the corner in Russian, before he arrives at his house, to be greeted in Gaelic or Greek by his neighbors, and finally in American by the housemaid, herself from Finland and proud of her command of the native lingo.

*

But I have forgotten to give you the smells of the city! So then, here is an inexhaustive list, drawn from my memory as I walked and gamboled and strolled here and there, eyes and ears open, absorbing the scent of the city in every pore.

Walk with me up Bush Street—uphill, I think, as we are fresh in the legs and the wind is at our backs. Up past Powell and Mason and Taylor, surely named for burly merchants or military men, or both at once, as is the American way; behind us the bells of Notre Dame des Victoires, a French Catholic church—the Marists, fine men with whom I have sipped many a glass; the best priests, in my opinion, appreciate the finer things in life, and do not shrink from that which the Creator has made, or allowed us to make from His largesse, like the swirling poetry of wine, and the meditative pleasure of tobacco.

Past Jones Street, where we pause for a cornucopia of scents: the faint wet burnt smell of laundry, the alluring aroma of coffee somewhere down on Sixth or Pine, the steady under-layer of coal fires burning to heat this drafty breezy city; the piercing smell of wood smoke and split wood, and perhaps ever so faintly the scent of the oils used to clean and preserve axes and hatchets and wood-wedges; the thorough smell of horse manure and hay and straw and horse sweat, and the drifting acrid scent of steam engines; a whiff of the beer and ale most residents drink every evening, even the younger ones—I have seen boys of twelve manfully quaffing their beer down at the docks, after a long day unloading boats and ships.

Past Leavenworth, Hyde, and Larkin, and now our legs are straining a little—it surely is a city of steeps and slopes, pitches and precipices, though I give no credence to stories of small dogs and toddlers slipping on Polk and rolling all the way down Bush into the bay; they would have slowed down sufficiently after ten or twelve blocks of hurtling along, so that a policeman or an enterprising preacher could have snatched them up; such legends are not to be countenanced, though occasionally I have seen carts and barrels hurtling down the street on their own, either lost by their owners, or breaking out at long last in coveted independence. It is that sort of country, where all things desire to be governed just a little, if at all; never was there a country like these United States, where independence is the common cry, dependence is the communal glue, and some sort of grudging interindependence a possible future; the whole nation is a kind of cheerful violent experiment in just how lightly the reins of government can lie upon the body of a people, without the commonality pulling apart in pockets of shrill rage and chaos. There are no robed kings and bewigged courts here, as the Americans are very fond of telling you, though they do have kings of their own kind, in lush offices and armed citadels, the former who dictate their will to underlings and shiver the markets at will, and the latter who obliterate the aboriginals, having no other enemy on which to exercise their armies.

Polk, Franklin, Gough—now we are along the spine of the city, as it were, and from our feet the west declines to the sea, the east to the bay. Again we pause to smell the wonderful symphony or cacophony of scents: the irresistible hint of ocean and sea-wrack and tide flat, the sharp pungency of pine and cypress and madrone, the tendrils of scent trailing after railroads and meat-packing and sugar-refining, even, perhaps, very faintly, an iota of cigar smoke, from the cheroots that every man and boy in San Francisco appears to burn from dawn to dusk. If we are fanciful we can say that we apprehend hints of opium and lust, which are sold freely in the streets, and certainly not just in Chinatown; and if we are more fanciful still we could say that we ascertain the slightest scents of the mounds of fish and produce that pour into the city every day, to be packaged and shipped right back out again in every direction. And do we smell the clink and sheen of money, the urge to power, the moans of the poor women who are prisoners to prostitution, the groans of the poor Asiatics who work the most and earn the least? Perhaps we do, perhaps we do; can it be so impossible to live and work and walk in a city of this size and bustle, and not see and smell and hear pain and despair, as well as thriving joy? You would be blind and deaf not to notice how a city is built upon the exhausted bodies of half its people; and this is true of all cities through history, from ancient Alexandria to tomorrow's Areopolis; even the cities we will someday compose in the sky will be built by poor strangers from another

planet altogether, perhaps—themselves confined at night to their squalid ghetto, as always was and always will be. Will we never be free of the urge to rank and to reign, to fawn at those above and sneer at those below?

★

Mrs Carson being away for a few days on a personal matter, the kitchen duties fell to Mr Carson, who accomplished them by the simple expedient of roasting deer meat over a fire, accompanied by pots of coffee; suitable fare for men in the wilderness, as Mr Carson said, which is where we were without the compass of Mrs Carson's shining presence to set us aright. The other residents in the house at that time being men of various burly occupations, used to rough fare and dense coffee, there was a convivial feeling in the kitchen, as if we were all a ship's crew, or a gang of timber-fallers, pleased to sit and eat by the fire at the end of a hard day, and tell stories of good times and bad.

Those few days I remember well for the sheer variety of stories, for the men in the house that winter were a wonderfully diverse lot, not only by their labor but by nationality, personality, and percentage of garrulity; one fellow from Russia was the most amiably verbose man I think I ever heard, a round sailor with an endless parade of tales from his years as a mariner, both with his country's navy and as an "agent of fortune," as he said; another man, from Ireland where all men are said to be natural raconteurs, was as lean and taciturn as the Russian was not; and of course, such being the way of the world, these two were the best of friends, and had shipped together for years in freighters and tramp steamers throughout the Pacific. As the Russian said cheerfully he did all the talking for the both of them during the year, except on the fourth day of March every year, which was Robert Emmet's birthday, when their agreement was that the Russian would strive to fast from words for a day, and the Irishman would speak freely, if not exactly at length, in honor of a great man among his countrymen, who only wanted freedom of thought and speech and judgment and religion for all, and strove incredibly to make a rebellion without shedding the blood *even of the oppressor.*

"He was captured by the imperialist soldiers only because he would not flee abroad without saying farewell to his beloved Sarah Curran," said the Russian, "and he was falsely tried by an imperial power who coldly bought off his cowardly lawyer, and they hung him, yes they did, right in the streets of his own beloved city, and then they cut off his head for good measure, being afraid of his ideas even after they killed him dead. But though his mortal remains be dust and wind today, his voice lives on and always will in Ireland, for every man, woman, and child, and verily the creatures of the earth and air and water there, know his last words, and can repeat them in a trice, so that they elevate and strengthen the hearts of those who would be free of their yoke. 'I acted as an Irishman, determined on delivering my country from the yoke of a foreign and unrelenting tyranny,' he said, staring up at the grim and furious judge. 'I wished to prove that Irishmen were indignant at slavery, and ready to assert the independence and liberty of their country. I am going to my cold and silent grave; my lamp of life is nearly extinguished; my race is run; the grave opens to receive me, and I sink into its bosom. But let no man write my epitaph. When my country takes her place among the nations of the earth, then, and not till then, let my epitaph be written. I have done.'"

We all sat silent for a moment, all seven or eight of us at table, and then the Russian turned to the Irishman and asked had he said it right, had he remembered it aright? But his friend had his head bowed down to his chest, and every one of us could see the sheen of tears on his face. Another silent moment passed and then John Carson rose and placed his hand on the man's shoulder. We all arose and did so also, some men very tenderly. It is a canard that rough men are rough all through; my experience is that very many men are like trees, rough-barked but clean and strong and true beneath exteriors shaped by hard weather.

7

THAT NIGHT, SITTING BY THE FIRE in the parlor, John Carson was, I believe, still moved by the Irishman's tears, for he told me a story that he said he had never told anyone, other than Mrs Carson, and never thought he *would* tell anyone, other than Mrs Carson, "to whom," he said, "I have told and will tell every fiber of my being, every iota of thought, every yearning and darkness in my heart, for as long as she will have me so forthright and unadorned, and still find some affection for me, though I be as honest as any man can be; for I will not hide anything at all from that woman. It would be a sin to be anything but naked in spirit with her, and hope that she still will love you despite her intimate knowledge, which might well turn another lover away. I am no heroic figure, but a man like any other, capable of selfish and selfless at once, of light and dark, courage and cravenness; all men are two men, always at war with each other, isn't that so? We don masks, we perform parts, we adopt personas, but we are never one sort of man, and not another. Even the greatest among us knows this to be so; perhaps the wisest among us are those

who admit it most easily. We have two arms, two legs, two ears, two eyes, two of most parts; why would we not have two sides to our characters, always wrestling with each other? A *life* is one thing we can see, a long grapple with love and money and pain and grace; but the other thing—the interior grapple—we do not see, though it be the wilder war; and what we account as character is not so much an achievement as it is a victory of the moment, the hour, the day. So even a paragon like Lincoln, or Grant, or my friend Mr Twain, or your countryman David Hume—by all accounts as great a man personally as intellectually—must grapple with his dark side, his lesser self, the greedy goblin inside every man. We wrestle in private, and beam in public; but you and I know that every man has two faces, and must strive all his days to be a better man than he knows he is."

I was startled to hear this phrased so well, for I had myself many times pondered exactly this, that every man *was* two men, and I had idly thought someday to try to write it out—indeed I had twice started a story on the theme, to no avail, and at the cost of a great deal of paper tossed into the fire. Although the failed efforts *had* been educational; the more I set myself to be an author, the more I realized that some stories would only allow themselves to be told in certain ways, and would not subject themselves to my command as to their shape and form and pace. I could only hope that they would impatiently await my further learning, and present themselves again when I had grown sufficiently in skill to unfurl them properly at last.

★

"I sat on that bench over the harbor in Sydney for a long time," said Mr Carson, "a long time—thinking about that interesting young man, and what he had said, and what he had seen in me, and spoken aloud; I had known it too, down in the innermost chambers of my heart, but had not allowed myself to admit and articulate it—who knows why? There are times that I think all the stories we tell of human beings are finally stories of making our way through the wilderness of ourselves, not through the wild world around us. So many tales of adventure and voyage and journey are finally stories of a subtle change inside a person, with the tumultuous passage of the body over mountain and desert and sea only an excuse, a drapery, a costume on something else altogether. Indeed sometimes I think everything that we do is some sort of theater; perhaps we need the aura of performance as a screen between us and naked feeling, so that we can sip it rather than be drowned by it. But you are the author, Mr Stevenson, and better able to come at such things with sentences; I am merely a maritime man, at work on the skin of the oldest story of all, the first story, the story from which all other stories come.

"I can say that my life changed direction on that bench, as if the bench was a boat, and when I sat down I was headed in one direction, and when I arose I was sailing on wholly another tack; I think I can say that fair. But before I could go in my new direction I had one last task in Australia, and that was to fulfill a promise I had made to a friend.

"This was a man called David, with whom I had shipped several times, a man I admired very much for his forthright honesty and gentle humor, his unswerving courage, and his remarkable ability to gather men together for a cause; I suppose that sort of man is often a leader in political or military or commercial arenas, but David had no ambition that way at all, and not because he was a brown man, an aboriginal man—*ab origine,* there from the beginning—but because he had no interest in gain, in the way that we usually measure it. His was the ambition of a moment and then another, is the best I can explain it. In our case, as shipmates, I saw him again and again take command of a crew not by rank or violence, but by the quality of his character; and each time this happened we were a much better crew, much more effective in our work, because we were pleased to be together, do you know what I mean? And that was his ambition, I believe—to solicit that from the people he met. He bound us together not in common awe of him but in a shy respect for what was best in ourselves—a thing that had not been called out of many men, before they shipped with David.

"His true name was not David, as I discovered. He had been born in a place called Gimuy, for the blue fig trees there, and he had been named Gurumarra, or dry lightning—a remarkably apt name, I should say, for the sudden flash of his ideas and his humor was exactly like the flicker of lightning on a day with no rain or thunder—illuminations arriving and leaving so quickly that you doubted your eyes and ears. He grew up by the sea and was entranced by it early, and set forth into it on boats as soon as he could. I had the sense from what he told me that his people were disappointed that he went to sea as a profession, as they thought him destined for some soaring achievement, but he never explained that aspect of his life. I can well imagine that he would have been a military visionary of surpassing skill had he bent his energies that way, and from what I understand of Queensland, the wars between residents and immigrants were more continuous and savage there than anywhere else on the continent. But I can better imagine that they thought him called to be a spiritual or national leader of rare power and energy—far more than a renowned shaman, and maybe something like a savior, the man to lead them out of tumult and into the country of peace. His gifts were all that way, and an author like you, Mr Stevenson, could write a hundred books of how his life there, had he stayed in the land of the blue fig tree, might have turned history in another direction altogether. I sometimes think of this myself, on days when the wind is from the southeast, and I fancy there is the rich tang of fig trees in the air; but maybe that scent is from one of our own hills, and not from the beaches where Gurumarra played as a child.

"Well, he died at sea, of course, as many of us do. I was there when it happened, and saw him vanish into the sea myself, never to be seen again, and perhaps someday I will tell you that story, for even his death was remarkable, and not a man who was there will ever forget it; occasionally I come across a shipmate from those crews, and the first and only thing we talk about is Gurumarra—I suppose in a sense he is still gathering us together, for every mate of mine from that time has changed the tack of his sails, and steers by the stars Gurumarra unveiled to him. The fact is, Mr Stevenson, that Gurumarra was a great man, whom the world did not, and does not, and will not know—but we who sailed with him know, and will not forget. A man's life, if he is lucky, creates a ripple in many other lives, and maybe that ripple grows and becomes a tidal wave; maybe.

"In the way of very good friends Gurumarra and I had sworn a vow together, that if death came for one, the other would care for his effects, and deliver his most precious things and messages to certain people. In large part to accomplish this I had shipped to Australia myself, though there were other reasons to sign with that particular ship and captain. In Sydney I had been paid off, and was for the moment solvent, with no lack of ships to join after I had fulfilled my vow. So when I arose from that bench, it was to find my way north to one particular beach, and there to deliver certain possessions and messages to Gurumarra's people.

"A long journey that was—up the coast, mostly, although here and there I wound my way inland, through long sunlit valleys and thick forests of gum and ironbark. I saw animals carved into rocks in remote mountains and caves—ancient lions, and kangaroos twice the height of a man; I fished and swam in many a hidden bay where I seemed utterly alone, although perhaps there were always watchers in the hills; I walked and rode wagons through dense wet forests and along quiet trickling rivers. I stood on hills and saw whales and tremendous turtles in the sea below me. The land was bright and brooding and wet and dry all at once; sometimes there would be storms of such voluminous rain that I would have to huddle in a cave or on a hotel porch for hours, and then make my way through mud fully a foot deep. Many people were friendly and helpful, a few remote and threatening, one or two actually dangerous; but I finally arrived in the town called Cairns, and delivered a box and two messages to Gurumarra's people, and a third message, to a boy of about ten years old.

"He told me that he had taken the name David, after Gurumarra came to him in a dream and told him to do so, and that Gurumarra had also said he was going to go into the belly of the ocean and explore there, and meet with the beings of the deep. He said that Gurumarra had appeared to him many times in dreams, about once a month or so. He said that Gurumarra was not dead in the way that I thought he was, but would not be able to meet me again in this life, but would meet me again in a next life, and would be delighted to see his old friend again.

"The boy David told me all these things as we sat amid blue fig trees on a sort of shelf above the beach; I think I will always remember his calm quiet voice, and his laughter when I pressed him about his dreams. 'I cannot tell you more,' he said, most politely, 'for that is not what Gurumarra asks of me. But I am to mark your skin, if you are willing to wear a story or message yourself—the scars are a gift from Gurumarra, and they will help you in some way I do not know. It is not my part to know.'

"I accepted this strange gesture, if you can call it a gift to have your chest and shoulders sliced with a knife, and I report that it hurt like the devil. What a scene that was! A whole group of men and boys around me on the beach, with watchfires burning, and the older men chanting and singing in their language, and me being carved gently but firmly by a fellow who could have been Gurumarra's twin brother, the resemblance was so close. A rare starry night there, they told me—I remember staring up at the sky, and seeing whole clans and tribes and seas of stars I had never seen before.

"The next day I put to sea in a little schooner trading down the coast to Brisbane and then to Sydney, and once back in Sydney I found a ship so quickly we were out to sea before my scars were healed. And soon enough I was back here in San Francisco, after a pause in the Sandwich Islands—yet another story for another day!—but now I was, as you might say, a marked man. What these markings mean I will never know, I think. But I do know that they are a message from my friend, the best man I ever knew, and so I wear them with reverence. How often, I ask you, does a man get to be the very page on which a story is written? Not so often, Mr Stevenson, not so often—and with that, I think we had best get to bed, for I must be up early, and you, I think, have many stories to write, and so you had best be about your dreaming. Remind me someday to tell you about my time in the Sandwich Islands, for that is a land of enchantment and music and scent unlike any other on this earth, I believe. Goodnight!"

★

By late February matters were both worse and better with me—worse in the way of health, which threatened sometimes to sink beneath the billows altogether, but better in the way of weddings; though Fanny too was ill for a time, and money was nowhere to be found, and our future as a family not illumined by substantial prospects for security, still, there was a gently waxing tide of hope. Her former husband was indeed now legally former, and happily removed from house and children, taking his crushing debts and ill repute with him to the bawdy houses and drinking clubs of San Francisco. The cottage in Oakland was slowly coming into her possession, conveyed by lawyers at their preternaturally glacial pace, half an inch per day, and back two inches on Sunday. The boy Lloyd does well in school, and lights up whenever he sees me, as I him; we speak the same language, he and I, perhaps because he is a quiet old soul, and I am always a capering boy inside the illusion of maturity. Fanny's girl Isobel seems happy enough with her lively husband Joe, although where they will find money enough to live peacefully is a mystery to all, and it seems to me that he sometimes likes his liquor more than anything else in his day; but it is certainly not my place, penurious soul that I am, to pepper young Mr Strong with admonitions and imprecations. As for my work, I am so nearly done with my book about my sea voyage to America that I should be writing of docking in New York City in the next two days; I am finished altogether and finally with a short novel about a prince that seems to me as good as anything I have done; and there is such a flurry of essays and stories and even poems floating about the workroom that I sometimes think all the seagulls of this most maritime city have come to visit at once, and whirl about the room in such numbers that I cannot easily distinguish bird from book.

But for the first time, as February began to dwindle and March hove into view, I found that even as I grew more sure that I would soon remove to Oakland, and marry the woman I adored, and begin a life together I had dreamed of now for five years, I would very much miss Mr and Mrs Carson, whose company had become so familiar and interesting and stimulating that when I contemplated its absence I was filled with sadness.

Even as I knew, or hoped with all my heart, that we would always be friends, and always exchange letters, and perhaps occasionally have the happy chance to meet, in California or Caledonia, I also knew that these hours by the fire with Mr Carson, as he unspooled his endless adventures in various corners of the world, and with Mrs Carson in the kitchen, as she shyly told of her own tremendous journey, her voice gentle and her hands never still, would stand alone in my memory as times of wonder, of absorption, of respect growing into something like reverence. Of all the remarkable men and women I have met in this life, I count the Carsons the most gracious, the least arrogant, and the most generous; and, happily for he who wishes with all his heart to be an author all his life, they were both filled with the most amazing and entrancing stories, which they shared as freely as they did the apparently inexhaustible supply of roasted oysters available to the lodgers every night at the dinner table.

It was oysters, in fact, which lured a remarkable story from Mrs Carson that month. I had worked furiously one afternoon to finish my voyage from Scotland to America, and on writing the last page, and clapping myself on the back at such heroic effort, I went downstairs for tea, and found Mrs Carson with a knife in her hand, and a barrel of oysters to be shucked. I was in an elevated mood; I could not bear to contemplate immediately plunging into my next book; and I suppose my unconscious mind saw a rare opportunity, for I took the shucking knife gently from Mrs Carson, and sat her down with a mug of tea and a mound of neeps to dice, and asked her to tell me two or ten of her stories, any ones she chose, as long as they were about her own life and journeys, for I was most curious about her own voyage to and across America, and from where she had started, and how she had come to harbor here on Bush Street.

"Well, now, Mr Stevenson," she said with a smile, "I am

not the raconteur that my John is, or a professional composer of stories like yourself, but if you are going to be so good as to shuck that whole barrel, I will indeed pay you with a story, and count it a fair exchange, for there is a solid hour of oysters there to be opened gently and gingerly; and if you will be careful, and not lose a finger in the process, I will tell a tale only John knows—consider it pried from me with the oyster knife.

"You know that I was long at sea, coming over and seemingly mostly *through* the Atlantic Ocean, and that I then made my way across the continent—though 'across the continent' is a phrase with three hundred stories in it, certain sure. I could draw you a map, or simply name the regions through which I traveled, and their names alone would be a sort of continental poem, don't you think? But let me tell you one story. A cold story, a story so bereft and frozen and despairing that did it finish that way there would be no teller of it today; but that is not the way it went, and all because of a strange peppery little man who was either mad, or a saint, or probably both.

"I waited long, when our ship docked, to make my way ashore. I was a stowaway, for one thing, and would surely have suffered from the sailors and officers, had they found me; and I was now an alien in a strange land, and female and penniless to boot, with not a word of whatever tongue they spoke here. I did not even know what country I was in, although I suspected, given the frigid temperature, that it was legendary Canada, to which many of the people of my native island had fled—Canada with its tremendous ghostly bears, and giant wet forests, and endless snow-scoured plains, and mountains so dense and remote no one even knew their extent. Some said it was always winter in Canada, and summer was only a holiday declared once a year, to appease residents who had heard of the idea, and thought their country ought to have a summer too.

"I slipped away from the ship before dawn, in that last hour of darkness during which even guards and sentinels sleep; and once off the dock I was indeed plunged into what seemed like the very lair of winter. There were walls of snow higher than my head in the streets, and alleys impenetrable with snow twenty feet high between buildings. Ice hung everywhere in the most fantastic spears and beards—some of the frozen drippings were ten feet long, and hung from the eaves of houses by the dozens and hundreds. There was ice in the roads, ice lining windows, ice coating stoops and steps and stairs—how the populace of the city managed to move about was a mystery to me, as I slipped and scrabbled my way through the empty silent streets.

"I was cold and hungry and so stiff and sore I would have wept, except that I was afraid my tears would affix a frigid mask to my face. I could not stop walking, for fear I would freeze right where I stood, and for fear a policeman would find me. But I knew no destination, no refuge, no friend, not even where I might find a fire and a bowl of soup; and it dawned on me that I was going to have to choose a door and knock on it and hope for the best. A church, a school, a tavern where I might find work in the kitchen—anything was better, I realized, than being found alone in the street when dawn came, for surely the first flood of residents would include sharp-eyed keepers of the law, or, even worse, citizens who, having survived their own struggle to respectability, are adamant in denying the chance to anyone else—every country has those citizens, and not all of them blustering men, either.

"So I chose a door, and knocked hard, and I think I will always remember that next long fraught and frightened minute; I stood there shivering, ready to run if need be, but hoping with all my might that a warm heart would be behind the hand on the lock. And I heard the lock being undone, and the door swinging open, and there was a flood of light and heat from behind the figure in the door . . . and what a figure it was!

"A *tiny* man, and I use the word advisedly; he was not five feet tall, with a bulbous nose, and a scatter of hair like a wren's nest, and a most forbidding expression; he looked annoyed and glowering and irritated, all stops on the way to furious. And then when he spoke! or more accurately *barked,* or growled, or snarled; the *sound* of his voice was so fearsome that I stepped back, but then I caught his meaning, which was, to my astonishment and relief, *come in.*

"I did not know his language, which I later found to be French—for I was indeed in Canada, and this was Montreal, and by happy chance I had knocked at a school, and this most unusual man was the door porter. I was to discover that he was also the school's barber, and janitor, and wagon driver, and carpenter, and bailiff, and metalsmith, and postal service, and nurse, and gardener, and wine steward to the faculty, and even, occasionally, grave digger—in short he did every job that needed doing except anything that entailed reading or writing, because he was illiterate, though he had tried with might and main to learn his letters.

"Well, he brought me into the kitchen, and indicated irascibly that I should sit by the fire, and then he brought me warm clothes, and steaming soup, and a loaf of the best bread I had ever eaten. As I sat by the fire, so stunned by fortune I could hardly think, it grew infinitesimally lighter outside, and I realized it was morning—my first morning in Canada, my first morning on land for a month, my first morning with hot food in my mouth for years.

"We think of a life as something composed of years, Mr Stevenson, but this is not so—this is not so at all. Our lives are made of moments, and not the vaulting ones that we think: the moment you are married, the moment you are a father, the moment you sell your book to the publisher, the moment you are sworn into office, the moment you unlock a new house. No—it's the sidelong moment that matters most, I think—the one no one would notice but you, because you felt the turn of the tide, the subtle depth, the shiver of wonder. I think the moments we remember best are the smallest ones. That moment by the fire was one of mine; a small moment by the measure of the world, but a mountainous one for me. It was the first moment someone had been kindly to me, for longer than I could remember, and I mark it well, and think of it often.

"I will stop there, for the story of that little man should be told with reverence and awe, and I see you are finished with the oysters. I should be up and about getting dinner ready, for oysters are best when they are freshest, and John will soon be home, as hungry as a sailor on Sunday. But do remember to ask me sometime for that little man's story, for I believe him to be one of the illuminated ones, the *soilsithe,* as my mother would say—the *menerangi,* John tells me they are called in Borneo. Every land is graced by the *soilsithe,* and how they arise from among us, and what strange and fantastic shapes they assume, and where they come from and where they go when they die is a great mystery; but were we more honest with each other than we are, we would speak more freely of them, for every one of us has met one or more, and knew it instantly, too. But we are so often afraid to speak of the things that mean the most to us, isn't that so? You of all men, being an author, would know that—isn't that why you write your books, in the end, to speak openly in print of the things we do not say aloud?"

*

This conversation with Mrs Carson stayed with me for days, and I spent many hours, as I walked about the city, pondering what she had said, and estimating the tidal moments in my own life, and then too of Fanny's life—the moment she knew her new husband was unfaithful, and would always and continually be so, for example; she said it was only the hint of a scent not his own, one night after a party at the commandant's house, that told her the whole tale, and turned her life, and that of their children, toward another point of the compass—east and north toward me, if I was being fanciful. . . .

I remember a whole day's walk, largely along the streets and wharves of North Beach, during which I meditated on just this thing, tidal moments in lives, and realized that so many books and stories depended on just such subtle targets for their energies; I had long thought of writing an adventure novel set in the Highlands of my hard and lovely homeland, for example, but could never see how to set the plot in motion, until that day, when I saw that something like the hero's sudden shocking kidnapping would set the prose to sprinting. In the novels of my countryman Walter Scott, in the wonderful books of Dumas, even in Shakespeare, the stories are set alight by a certain fraught moment—a grim injustice that ripples into many other lives, the first flash of madness in an otherwise reasonable king, the instant when Prince Hal must forsake the companion he loves the best, if he be the man he must.

Long I walked that day, and even now, many years and miles away from those windy wharves and stony streets, I remember the weather, and the surge of wild current through the Gate, and the faintest clatter of wagons and marching men from the Presidio, and the rough music of many languages along the water's edge—I thought I could make out

Portuguese and Spanish, and Russian and Finnish, and Chinese, and a dozen accents of English and American, and even once, I thought, the round soft burr of my own Scottish—an in-between tongue, Scottish is, still half wild ancient Scots Gaelic and half the imperial English that rose from my home island to take much of the world. I spun on my heel and sought for that voice for almost an hour, to no avail, and finally walked back up to Bush Street, homesick for the first time in many months. I had come halfway around the world to marry Fanny, and here I was alone, still unmarried, still unknown, still counting pennies desperately every morning to see if there were enough for bread with coffee. But I did have good friends, I realized, not one but two; and I had been slathered beyond all expectations with unforgettable stories, which are better than bread, for a writer; and I had hopes, high hopes, of a life with the woman I loved most in this life, though she be across the bay, which sometimes seemed nine oceans wide to me, in the hours when I was weary, and there was no wind to fill my sails.

8

ONE FINE DAY A FRIEND OF MINE from my stay in the Carmel Valley stopped up in San Francisco to see me, and in the course of a long morning's perambulations we fetched up along the wharves on the north side of the city, whereupon a fisherman he knew pressed a tremendous salmon upon him, as payment of some sort of ancient debt; my friend attempted, laughing, to decline the payment, or at least postpone it for another time when he might have a cart or a sturdy son to bear the fish home, but the fisherman would not be denied, and who, in the end, can argue with the gift of a tremendous fish? Even Our Blessed Lord loved fish, as you remember, and conducted miracles with fish, and asked for fish as His first meal when awakened from the tomb. So finally we accepted the fish, and made a remarkable spectacle of ourselves carrying it home to Bush Street. Picture a gaunt young Scot, thin as a stick with a jacket, and a scrawny leathery man, aged seventy-two, the two of us together weighing surely less than our increasingly redolent burden, and you will see why we caused uproar and merriment all the way back to Mrs Carson's, where we considered that the salmon would meet his or her most savory fate.

My friend stayed for dinner, at Mrs Carson's invitation, and well he did so, for not only did they get along famously, but his occupation—he was a bear hunter, and by all accounts a famous one up and down the California mountains—led to a story from Mrs Carson that unlocked a great puzzle for me. But let me set the scene properly, and give my friend Anson his own inimitable voice, and let his story lead to hers, as would happen in a proper book, were there such a thing as a Proper Author hereabouts to make one.

"I was in a revolt, miss," said Captain Smith, for that is what the world called him, whether he actually had been appointed captain under Colonel Fremont or not, "but that was when I was youngish, and California was a part of another country, and there were those of us who wished it to be its *own* country, which it was, briefly, and sometimes now I think the republic lasted only as long as the few days we raised the bear flag over it. But that was long ago, and since then I have concluded that there is no such thing as a country, really; there's only groups of people living as best they can, and what we call countries is generally an excuse for men to take money they did not earn from those who did earn it. Myself now I have a ranch, running goats with a friend of mine from the wars, and it seems to us that the ranch is a country itself, for we have a healthy population of children and goats and deer and badgers and bears, and we vote on matters, and exact taxes, which is to say deer and trout and quail, and we stand to arms if necessary to protect the citizenry—just did so recently, in fact, when a fellow came through our country thinking that he could freely remove the furs from a number of our residents. We deported him, after undiplomatic negotiations. Also we have a lion-hound, and no man ought argue with a dog that will track a lion. There are not so many of that kind of dog, you know.

"But me, I am a bear hunter, and there are not so many of us either, for the cinnamon bears here are going up into the mountains to get away from people, and the golden bears, the biggest bears in the world, I believe, are losing their war against people who shoot them for hardly any good reason. The only decent reason to kill a golden bear is if he is eating your animals, and even there he has a good case that you and your animals are on his land and not the other way around; his people were there long before your people were, is how I look at it. But they do be hunted, and I figure if he has to be hunted he might as well be hunted by someone who knows and respects him, and does the job fair and just, and doesn't just shoot him to take his fur off, or leave him there stinking for the condors. So my pal and I, we do some bear hunting, and to be honest it gets us off the ranch and into the woods and away from the goats, which is an obstreperous animal altogether.

"Now, the real bear hunters up and down the coast, we know each other, because we are a sort of a tribe ourselves, with certain rules and customs and traditions, and we respect the best among us, and tell stories of them and their adventures, especially with particular bears. There was the San Luis

Rey River bear, for example, who fought all day long and knocked down an old oak tree he was so angry, and the Santa Clara River bear who weighed a lot more than a ton. But it's not always the biggest bears. There was a lean old golden bear up toward Sonoma Creek north of here who never did get shot, though many a man hunted him; it is said that he was a master at hiding behind trees, and there's some even think he could *climb* trees, and there are even stories that he could change his color to disguise himself depending on what tree he was in, although I don't think that's a true story, myself.

"Similarly there are stories of hunters who are famous for whatever reason. We tend not to like fellows who shoot a lot of bears, though that sort of fellow thinks he ought to be famous, but being famous for causing a lot of death isn't much to be famous for. For us it's more the story. There's an old woman in the Siskyou mountains up in Oregon country who can track bear better than anyone I ever saw; she was down here once tracking a bear who liked to use the tide to wipe his footprints on the beach. That was one smart bear. She found him, though. And there's a young Okwanuchu fellow in the Shasta River country who we think is very fine, and two brothers up in the Nisqually River country who are the best hunters up that way, and there's a few fellows in the Canada forests who are very fine hunters. Now up there the bears change, and are not so golden, but they can get even bigger, and the best hunter is a fellow who personally fought a terrific bear not once but several times, until they finally agreed to call their duel a draw."

132

At this Mrs Carson exclaimed aloud, and asked for more details, and Captain Smith said, "Well, he is a most *hairy* man, miss, and there's some who call him Harry or Hairy as a sort of joke, though those of us who know him would never jest at his expense; he is a most gentlemanly and kindly man, and what he has not done for his neighbors can't be reported, for there's nothing he has not done for them, by their own account."

"He wears a bear claw on a string around his neck?" said Mrs Carson.

"Indeed he does, miss," said Smith. "From the very bear he fought, the bear who extracted a tooth from him in exchange, or so he says; and if *he* says it, it's so."

"But I know him, esteem him as much as you do," said Mrs Carson with a smile, and it was wonderful to see the look of surprise flood across the captain's seamed face; it is always a pleasure to see words that entered ears be instantaneously transformed into a flicker on someone's face; a subtle and lovely thing.

"He is indeed a most kindly man," continued Mrs Carson, "and his name is Gérard Harrison, which is why some people call him Harry, and everything he says is true, and he once helped me escape a great danger, and that is a story that has a great deal to do with bears, and I will tell it to you sometime, if you like. But our tremendous salmon is ready to consume, and it would be disrespectful both to fish and fisherman to not make the most of such a gift. Shall we to table?"

★

Reading over what I have written thus far of John Carson's adventures, I see that Mrs Carson's adventures are coming up fast along the rail behind her husband's, and that the author himself, and the woman he loves, are far more of a presence than I had envisioned; I never meant this to be a tale of four people, but a sketch of one remarkable man. Also I notice that many other people are strolling in and out of the story just as they please—on just a casual glance over the pages here on my desk, I find Mr Mark Twain, and a dog named Lazarus, and Mr Alfred Wallace, and a boy named Adil, and a Dayak chieftain in Borneo called Pale Hawk, and Miss Frances Matilda Vandegrift Osbourne, and a girl in a stone village on the shoulder of a mountain in Ireland, and a Catholic priest who was rescued from a hell of the soul by Mr Carson, and the young sailor in Sydney whose piercing words sent Mr Carson sailing in wholly another direction in life, and a Yidingji man called Gurumarra, or Dry Lightning; and this is not even to mention such brief visitors to our book as the actor with a trunk packed with the costumes of Cicero and Pericles and Demosthenes, or the man from Canada who wore a bear claw around his neck.

This panoply or plethora or procession of visitors is not something I had expected, but I find that I cannot keep them out: they insist on telling at least a bit of their stories, and the cleverest ones persuade me easily that their story materially advances or augments that of John Carson, who was to be our primary subject. Indeed, as the priest noted, perhaps John Carson is best understood as a sun around which other galactic bodies revolve, each of the latter then in some occasional relation with each other, by virtue of their original relation to the magnetic force at their center. This makes some sense to me, if we understand that John Carson had not the slightest inclination to power or influence, control or authority; indeed, it was the very absence of those common driving forces in other men that perhaps made him so interesting to so many.

In my experience, the men who affect *not* to care of the opinions of others care very much indeed, and actively solicit your good opinion of their ostensible lack of caring about that very thing. Conversely there are many men who so desire your good opinion, that they will be at strenuous and insistent pains to tell you clearly why you should esteem them so—for their strength, their wit, their acumen, their money, their status, their beauty, their courage, their intimacy with God, or, best of all, the high opinions held by men of whom *they* have a high opinion; the men of whom I speak are in a sense always brandishing testimonials about themselves in the public square, often so loudly and assiduously that I have come to suspect that they do not themselves believe what it is they shout to the rooftops.

All this, on either side, was not John Carson's way. He was at once the most generous and the least interested of men; he would, as I saw for myself on many occasions, give away his money and labor without the slightest hesitation, but never think for a moment of repayment, or future favor, or whether or not your project was sensible, and his time well spent. If you asked, he was your man; if you were in need, he was your man; if you did not ask, and did not need, he was more than content to conduct his own affairs in and out of the house. I sometimes thought that *because* he evinced no interest in social matters, he was eagerly sought out by a certain class of men in San Francisco; with my own eyes I witnessed invitations proffered him by the habitués of clubs, by men of business, by men of the cloth, by men of political ambition, but in all cases he declined. He did so with a wonderful grace, so that each of the men who were asking him for his time so as to be associated with him, and thus be able to trumpet his good opinion, left the room thinking he had acquired just that; but I noticed that John Carson never once, that I knew, joined any group, or club, or church, or party. You would think the clear record of his reluctance in social matters would dissuade further invitations, or at least cause them to wither to a trickle, but this was not so; the cards and letters arrived at such a rate that every other week Mrs Carson would use them to spark the fire, and comment pleasantly on the way that the ones with wax seals added color and zest to the flames.

What *did* Mr Carson do with his days? To be direct, how did he make his living? One night, along about the end of February, I asked him this forthright, feeling that we were close enough friends now that I could inquire without rebuff, and he laughed and delivered a brief merry speech that has stayed in my memory ever since, for the blunt cheerfulness of it.

"For one thing, Mr Stevenson, I do not own this house— Mrs Carson does, and you and I both reside here at her pleasure; so I do not have to pay a note, or a landlord, or a tariff to a grandee somewhere. She owns the place free and clear, and there is a story in that for you someday, though you must hear it from Mrs Carson herself, for some stories belong only to one teller, and they have no weight or substance in the mouth of another.

"As for me, other than my work around this house for its shipshape upkeep, I am a maritime man still, and am in the business of men and ships. At one level I suppose I could say that I am in the way of connecting men and ships, putting men on and taking them off, moving one to another as fate and circumstance dictate—for the right man on the right ship matters tremendously, and many a ship and journey and venture has faltered or foundered because the right men were on the wrong ship, or the right ship was staffed by the wrong men. And only a little of such dissonance is enough to cause a problem. So part of my job is to ease such dissonance, and measure men and ships, and do my best to put one man on a yawl and another on a schooner, one brother on a sloop and his twin on a steamer; for men are just as different as ships, and how they weather storms, and how they handle in high winds, and how grim their resolve when all is dark, and how much they will steal when no one is watching—these are things to be discovered only by living, for no man knows his own character until it endures some dirty weather. That is one true thing I have learned from my years at sea.

"I am also in the way of being a bayman, I suppose you could say—not in the sense of the fellows fishing the bay in their little sloops and skiffs, the scallop draggers and the

oystermen—no, here too I am in the business of connecting
men and ships in one part with men and ships in another.
We forget that the bay is not one entity, but five: Suisun Bay
and San Pablo Bay, north and south San Francisco Bay, and
the mother of waters to whom they report in the end, the
vast bay, as it were, of the ocean, waiting hungrily beyond
the Golden Gate. Each of these great waters has its particular flavors and characters, residents and migrants, styles and
manners, and my work, or a good part of it, is to shepherd
the catch in Suisun Bay, for example, to certain wharves and
canners in the city, and then away on ships to all points
west. Such transactions need middlemen to pick and choose
at either end of the trade, and I am one of those men in the
middle. In a way I suppose you could say that I am that lucky
sort of man who understands various languages, and can accept information in one and translate it productively to another; I speak clam and mussel and oyster, and shrimp and
turbot, and herring and cod, and stevedore and chandler,
and boatswain and owner, and I walk and wander and visit
and listen, and I know whom to trust and whom to avoid, and
who will deliver his catch on time and properly cleaned and
who will add gravel to gullets, and who stood by his mates
in a storm in Sumatra and who cowered in his bunk pretend-
ing to be sick, so that when I am asked about men in any
sort of capacity, I can with confidence provide an answer—
and there is a living in the right answer, for me, at least.
Though if ever there was a man who was paid less in coin
and more in fish it would be myself—just yesterday we ate a

goodly number of the answers I gave a man who paid me in oysters."

Did he like the work, did he love it?

"If I cannot be at sea, I can with great pleasure be near it," he said, after a moment; it was interesting to see him pause and ruminate a little before he spoke. "I will not be *expeditious* anymore, I think, but I can adventure all day along the water, and often on it—I suppose every other day I am on the water somewhere, checking on sturgeon in Suisun, or salmon pouring through the bay toward the Sacramento River, or whales cavorting by Point Diablo. Men and ships, fish and animals, wind and weather, rigging and rudders—I do love the work, because it *isn't* work, for me; it's what I would do with my hours and days anyway. Here and there, once a month or so, I feel the old urge to be aboard and away, and I'll watch boats slide past Lands End, and wish, for a moment, I was with them, cursing at sea lions in our wake, snarling at the new men, checking the rigging for the third time in an hour; but then I remember that a hundred times the pleasure of what I might find at sea is waiting for me on Bush Street, and up the hill I walk, to this very kitchen, where Mrs Carson is captain of all she surveys, and I might find, if I am lucky, strangers from every land on earth, including, if you can believe it, a most inquisitive Scotsman, cheerful of mien and thin as a sail no matter how much good food Mrs Carson endeavors to provide. And speaking of dinner, I believe tonight we are dining on a San Mateo sturgeon that weighed more than you do before its demise last night; it is the answer to a question about which men from the Mission District would and would not be right for an expedition to Alaska. Shall we?"

★

On the last day of February, 1880, I received news of not one but two stories accepted by a London magazine, with payment to come posthaste; I received notice that not one but two essays had been accepted by newspapers, which do not pay as well or as promptly but they *do* pay eventually, bless their inky hearts; and I received a letter from my dear friend Sidney Colvin, reporting, with the genuine and heartfelt pleasure in another's joy that is the keel of the admiration I feel for him, that my father, Thomas Stevenson, who had until this time objected to my prospective marriage to Fanny, has relented in his opinion, and will be pleased to send us small but steady money on a monthly basis, with his best wishes and those of my mother, who forebore to try to sway my father's opinion, having long experience in the impossibility of such a task.

I was delighted; I capered about my little room at the top of the house; I threw open the window, and shouted joyful noises to the streets below, terrifying a passing crow in the process; I ran down the stairs as helter-skelter as a child at Christmas, to share the news with Mr and Mrs Carson, and any stray lodger who happened to be in the kitchen or parlor; and then I rushed from the house down to the docks, to take the first ferry to Oakland, and share the extraordinary news with Fanny; for this changed everything for us, and lifted us from worry to merry—we would be able to marry, we would be able to care for her son, we would be able to go home to Scotland, and then live where we would—England? France? New York? Zanzibar? The world was open to us now, and we would finally be a family, and not a gaunt and penniless suitor at the door of a woman whose first and last concern, properly so, was her children.

I could have flown over the bay myself unaided, such was my transportive joy; and I chafed at the bow of the boat, and harried the captain under my breath for his sloth, until finally it touched home on the quays of Oakland, and I shot up the hill fast as a falcon, to the little cottage where Fanny lived.

I realize just now that I have mentioned Fanny a hundred times in this account, and told you where she was born, and said something of her wastrel husband, the charming and thoroughly adulterous Lieutenant Osbourne, and of her children Isobel and Lloyd, but I have told you nothing of who she *is*—her wit, generosity, verve, magnetism—the aspects and virtues that compose the actual person.

Fact and appearance are *useful* things, to be sure, and they outline only a perimeter of understanding, a rind on the real—so that if I tell you that she was born in the middle of America, and married the dashing lieutenant when she was all of seventeen, and she was instantly pregnant with Isobel, and all too soon aware that her husband was not who she thought him to be, that tells you something of her young beauty, of her headlong will, and of how she was forced to maturity sooner than most—but it tells you little of who she *is*.

So let me try. She is small and forceful. She is tender and flinty. She loves her daughter Isobel with all her heart and soul and they bristle around each other like rancorous cats. She loves her son Lloyd with all her heart and she broods over him and weighs him down with her fearful and overweening love. She lost a third child, a little boy, Hervey, only five years old, buried in an obscure grave in France, and I see her haunted by him sometimes; she croons wordlessly sometimes, when she thinks she is alone and unnoticed, and I know she is keening for her little boy; I have even seen her rock him in her arms too, when she was very sick with fever herself, and her mind was wandering through her previous lives.

I sit here in my study and write the words *love* and *attraction* and *intimacy of heart* and *companion of the soul* and they are the leakiest and most untrustworthy of vessels for what I mean. They cannot contain but a trace of my intent and they are instantly overthrown by the weight of intimation. Yet what have I to use but these poor tools? She is not pretty, by the estimation of this world, but she is beautiful. She is not charming, or so say some of my dearest friends, yet she is magnetic in ways that make me stammer. She never went near a university, but she is brilliant; she never had more than a few dollars on the table, yet she raised three children alone; she will never win accolades for her social sheen, yet she was instantly the alluring center of every social circle in which she found herself. She has a temper like a hurricane, a cyclone, a tornado, but you would endure that withering blast with a smile twice a day, just to be near her. To what can I compare her that would give you any true sense of her remarkable character and personality? The sun, I suppose—bright and hidden, warming and burning, as necessary as food, as mysterious as to its origins and purposes as the incomprehensible Imagination that spoke it into being and set it alight in the sky.

All of which is to explain a little, perhaps, of how I felt, strolling up her cottage path in Oakland, past the riotous flowers, and calling for her, and catching young Lloyd as he sprinted headlong from the house and plowed into me, happy as a hound; and there she is in the doorway, smiling; and all is well, and all manner of things will be well.

March 3, 1880, Oakland

My dear Louis,

This seems so strange to write a letter, when I could take the ferry across and see you in a few hours, or you could be here similarly swiftly, as a few days ago; but often I feel that I am more articulate on the page than anywhere else, and I want to try to say some things that are immensely important to me; things you know, but I want to get them down, get them onto the page and into your heart.

You saved me, beloved; and not in any way the world

will see, with money and houses and travels, though those things may someday come, given your extraordinary talents and relentless labors. *You saved me.* I was lost and you found me, and your love brought me back to life, and I can never thank you enough. I was dry, Louis; I was desiccated, and shriveled, and parched, and never again did I think it would rain, never again could I even imagine being loved for myself, as a woman, as a being who just wanted to be witnessed, apprehended, perceived, let alone savored and perhaps even loved; I was even happy alone, because I had the children, though we had lost blessed little Hervey. *We* meaning Isobel and Lloyd and me, the family of us three—I will not even speak or write his name who abandoned us so thoroughly, so continually, so smilingly, never again will I write his name, and if God is good to me I will someday forget it altogether—and then smile at having finally been released from the prison of marriage to him—if it ever was a marriage at all.

All the rest of my life, Louis, I will remember you leaping through that window, as I sat to dinner with the other guests in the hotel; all my life I will remember you sweeping off your hat, and bowing low with the grace and humor I would come to know so well, and saying exactly the right warm witty thing, and staring at me with your eyes like fire, like stars, like embers, like pools of light; and everyone was laughing, and in an instant your cousin had whisked you away, and slowly the world returned to what it had been, a dinner party, a bevy of guests, the evening breeze through the trees outside; but I stood there, Louis, and I was a different woman after that moment; and I have been a new woman ever since.

It is easy enough to write the words *I love you*, but impossible for me to explain how very deeply and thoroughly and excitedly I mean them, with every fiber of my being. When we are married and you are the husband and father you so wish to be, I will be happier than any woman who ever walked this earth. Sometimes it seems so terribly far off that our wedding day will come, with so many travails to surmount; but then there is a night like this one, when I feel your love like a bonfire across the bay, and for a moment it seems like perhaps tomorrow is the day we stand together and vow our lives to each other forever.

All my love, Louis my dear, and Lloyd sends his affection, and says he is working hard on his newspaper, and wishes that you would contribute "two columns of leader, and one poem, of no fewer than twenty lines, with a drawing if you feel like it," his exact words.

Your loving
Fanny

In early March the house on Bush Street had another visitor from Mr Carson's past, and this distinguished gentleman was of such a gentle and courteous nature, and so intellectually curious, and so riveting in the way that his ideas leapt up to hold hands with yours and sprint off into new and unexpected fields of inquiry, that when our long conversation by the fire was concluded, I went upstairs to my room and made notes of what I could remember; for I knew instantly that here was not only a rare mind among the people of the earth, but an even rarer case of a silver intellect directed by a most genial and disegotistical soul. The combination is remarkable, and did we measure men by what we ought to, that is to say their true qualities, and not muscle or money or magnetism, here would be a leading citizen of the age; but Mr Carson tells me, and Mr Wallace confirmed it with a broad smile, that he is not very famous at all, in other than a very small circle of people who believe his scientific ideas to be not only revolutionary but right—two very different things, and the latter not at all as alluring as the former, in the general course of worldly matters, as Mr Wallace noted.

He was at this time in America only briefly, on his way home from a scholarly speaking tour, and had stopped in San Francisco expressly to meet Mrs Carson, of whom he had heard much in correspondence but had not the honor of her acquaintance, "as I am almost always now in England, and no longer a man of the world, and not at all the man you remember, John, wandering about in the mud, gaping at insects, and being saved from death and disaster by such able fellows as you and Charles and Adil—that was more than twenty years ago now, although I still dream of the jungles, and see my butterflies and flying-frogs in the glimmer, and hear the coughing of leopards not far away . . . I imagine

I am the only man in Surrey nowadays who startles at leopards, and surreptitiously looks for a stick with which to defend himself from a possible charge—surely I am the very picture of an odd old man of the district, whom schoolchildren point out to their fellows as the local madman."

His talk, his talk! Over the course of the evening he talked about the vast wilderness of Amazonia, and how it was there he began to suspect that perhaps rivers were barriers that finally dictated, over uncountable thousands of years, the shape and form and habits of certain animals. He talked about how he began to realize, ever so slowly, "painfully and embarrassingly and ashamedly slowly," that aboriginal peoples were not in any way inferior to "civilized" peoples, and in fact were often to be much admired for their moral and intellectual and spiritual integrity. He talked about his beloved orang-utang, "a most remarkable being, for any number of reasons, but that is a discussion for a whole month of evenings by the fire, which I do hope will someday come to pass, should you and your new bride be passing through Surrey in your authorial perambulations, Mr Stevenson." He talked about his correspondence and respect and friendship with Mr Charles Darwin, whom he much admired and very graciously credited as the first to imagine the theory for which both men were now famous; "certainly Mr Darwin thought of the idea first, years before I had the happy chance to stumble upon it," he said, "and rather than contest priority and primacy, I much prefer to be amazed that two young fellows should hit upon the same remarkable idea half a world apart, and then, by the happiest of chances, become friends—that is much more interesting, and important, than who did what when, don't you think?" He talked about all sorts of birds, not only his beloved birds of paradise but the lowliest wrens and finches in his garden, "for the latter fit their place in just as wondrous a fashion as the former, though we think one surpassingly beautiful and the other common; but the wrens do not think wrens are drab, and perhaps there is much to be learned from their perception." He wondered about the many races of human beings, and why they adopted certain forms and colors and patterns of existence, and wondered aloud if perhaps there had been many other species of human beings, or nearly human beings, whose existence did not survive various stresses and situations in the tremendous yaw of the unknown past. He waxed eloquent about the colors of birds in particular, and wondered if some colors were designed by nature to draw attention, and some to deflect attention, and some to hide the bearer, and some to broadcast and advertise messages, as it were—this line of talk fascinated all of us, and it was Mrs Carson who spoke most feelingly and fervently about color and cloth, and perception and illusion, and costumery and class, and how the smallest detail of dress and grooming spoke volumes to those who paid close attention to such things; which would be all women and most men, she said, which drew a roar of laughter from Mr Wallace, who had hung on every word, and even asked if he might make notes on what she had said, so that he could consider her penetrating ideas slowly and fully on his voyage home to England.

There was much else said that night—we talked about Mr Wallace's books, and how he had actually written the story of Adil and Mr Carson in his book about the Malay achipelago, but seen it stricken from the manuscript by an editor who insisted the book stay in its strictly scientific channel; we talked about migratory patterns in birds and animals and human beings; we talked about what effect human beings might even now be having on a world that knew them not for untold years, but now "*endured* us," in Mr Wallace's word, in every corner of the globe; we talked about languages and music and cities and ships and islands and novels and Scotland and marriage and the "very real possibility, even perhaps probability," as he said, "that a semblance of the same scientific conditions that provoke life on this planet may exist elsewhere in the unimaginable reaches of space, which would have absolutely fascinating implications as regards new species, manners of existence, languages, and the like—imagine untold thousands of new kinds of music! Imagine places where eyes and legs are reversed, or trees speak, or everything alive is of a maritime character. . . ."

And one more moment I remember vividly from that night. Picture Mr Wallace, with his tremendous beard, standing by the fire—a tall man, slender, now beginning to stoop a bit. He was speaking ostensibly to all three of us, Mr and Mrs Carson and myself, but it seems to me he was really speaking directly to Mrs Carson when he said, "You will know the respect that so very many people hold for John, the universal esteem with which he is remembered on the island; and not just for his rescue of the boy, though that is a dramatic tale that encapsulates his obdurate courage and grace. There is much else to tell, and little time to tell it, and the words I have are thin for what I wish to say. He was kind; he worked hard and well and without a word; he was gentle; he was fair and honest; he treated each being in just the same way, with a grave attentiveness that spilled easily into laughter, if it could. Even then, not much more than a boy himself, you could see the man being formed, and knew the man to be your good and true friend, as long as life—the sort of man you could come to, at any hour of the day or night, wherever he chose to make his abode, and there ask him for help, and his help would be given freely and instantly and without the slightest hesitation, to the pinnacle of his considerable powers of body and mind. I do not know that there is a greater thing in a man than that sort of instantaneous assent to service, without quail or cavil; we all aspire to that, but the mass of men will weigh and measure, gauge and consider, appraise and assess, estimate and project, before they will step forth with a will—but not John Carson.

"I have lived long enough now to observe men in something of the way I have spent so many years studying animals," continued Mr Wallace, "and I conclude that the true measure of a man is nothing you can see with your eye at all. The adornment, the size, the coloring, the songs of romance and combative challenge, the striving for rank and status and power—those are things you can notice and record and categorize; but kindness and tenderness, patience and grace, courage when no one will know, integrity when no one will see, creativity when none will witness and applaud—those are the things that make a man, or not.

"I honored John, when he left the island, in the only way I knew, and appended his name, in the Latinate, to a creature new to science. A tiny frog, hardly bigger than the point of a pencil, which lives, so far as I could tell, in pitcher plants—*Nepenthaceae,* a sort of open gourd, from which monkeys drink water after rain, and called by some of the jungle people *kantong semar,* Semar's pockets, after a cheerful deity from ancient times. I do not suppose that there are more than four or five people in the world who know of the tiny frog *Carsonia* in the upland forests of Sarawak; but tonight we add three to this small society, those who study our lively cousins the frogs, themselves descended from the same animating force that set the stars to spin, and life to whirl from one form to another, arriving at, in its turn, us. And who knows if there will always be an us? One can hope so, we can certainly hope so; and most of all we can hope that whatever that future us will be, it will be composed largely of the best of us now."

I believe it was soon after this that we concluded the evening, and went to our rooms, and in the morning Mr Wallace was away and gone already, home to his garden in Surrey; but I think I will remember that evening and that soaring and delightful talk all the rest of my days. Affable and lively, free and fluid, informed and curious at once, harmonious and humorous both; reflective of the man and his mind, but no mere sermon or homily or pat pronouncement; eager to apprehend another mind, but not subservient or squelch-able; airy and open, darting and discursive, amicable and passionate together; ruminative and energetic, stimulated by company and concourse; musical, in a sense, in that he played variations on themes he knew, but never the same song twice; riverine, serpentine, sinuous, rushing along all a-tumble but, at the same time, channeled and bounded and headed to a specific point. His learning and erudition were staggering, but there was not a jot of pompous in him, nor desiccation, nor professorial arrogance; and he was thirsty for the ideas and opinions of others, not the sort of man who waits impa-tiently for another to finish before he launches forth his own cascade. An expert in his chosen field, but no urge to impose his faith upon you; no gossip and no verbal combat did he offer; indeed he was not interested, that I noticed, in verbal victory, as much as he was in the exploration of new territory, the acquiring of wider knowledge through the studies and stories of other beings. Eloquent and lucid, limpid and hu-morous, poignant and luminous; and finally he was most interested in celebrating another, not in being celebrated himself, though he surely had cause to be, given what only he and one other man in history had perceived of the unimag-inable workings of uncountable lives through immeasurable years. A most remarkable man; the sort of man I wish to be, of whom it might someday be said, that he was much more than his worldly accomplishments, whatever they should turn out to be; a man mourned much less as a lost artist, than as a good and true and beloved husband, and father, and friend.

9

March 3, 1880, Bush Street, San Francisco

My dear Colvin,

I set pen to paper this morning to give you a strict sense
of the actual conduct of my days, which are such a
blizzard of paper and dreams and walks and stories and
sharp winds and oysters and the scent of salt water that I
sometimes feel that I am a seaman charged with keeping
the log all day in a pitching schooner far out to sea; but
instead I find myself absorbed with the idea of being
a father, so to speak, to a boy I hardly know. This is
young Lloyd Osbourne, with whom I have forged a
happy bond based in silliness and theatrical prance—a
persona I know all too well, having lived many years in
it myself as a young man—*you* will remember the
poseur poet of the alleys of Edinburgh, always eager to
shock and startle his parents, to drink the cup of sordid
experience, to pretend with all his might to be a flaneur,
an idler, a hail-fellow-well-met without a shilling to his
name, or the prospect of one—how I wasted those

years, Colvin, how I burned away the hours in drinking and flirting and trying so very hard to not be what my father wished me to be! Such heroic effort *not* to be someone, when I might have spent the same effort trying *to* be someone; but now I am hard at work doing that very thing—note the enclosed two essays, one story, one meandering article, two poems, and one excellent drawing of myself losing a beloved hat yesterday on California Street—how apt and fitting that part of me should be carried away by California! For that is what has happened, and will happen, I pray—I will be carried away by a Californian, or two, if we count Lloyd, as we must.

He is a charming boy, shy and dreamy, like, perhaps, I was, and we get along famously—in large part perhaps because he and I much enjoy sprawling on the carpet, and doodling and drawing, and inventing islands, and imagining ourselves jungle explorers, and assigning ourselves various majestic titles, the Exalted Poobah of this and the Chief Mate of that—all to Fanny's distraction and dismay, for I think sometimes she looks at the two of us laughing on the floor and wonders if she is acquiring another headlong boy, rather than a stalwart husband. But she is secretly pleased, I know, that Lloyd and I share common ground; and I suspect she is pleased also that I have no interest in authority over either of them. My concern is to support and protect them, not direct or command; I am hardly in command of myself, after all, and it would be hullabaloo should I ever attempt to instruct anyone else in anything at all.

To you confidentially I will confess that I lay awake more often than I would like, pondering even this sort of once-removed fatherhood; it will be complicated and mysterious enough to try to be a decent and attentive husband to Fanny, who deserves exactly that, and I am not thoroughly confident that I can be that man all day every day. But I hope for the best: I love her and she loves me, and we want to exalt each other, and be of every assistance in the other's elevation; she understands my hunger to write such books as were never composed before in this world, and I understand her own creative desires—though what form they will take is a mystery all round. She *wants* to write, she *does* occasionally write; but it is that word "occasionally" that is the sticky wicket, between you and me. I do not think that someone who dabbles in the inky art will ever find the deep reaches you can touch sometimes with hard and steady work, the days when you are astonished by what has leapt from your pen, the moments when you look up, after some hours of absolute concentration, and realize that the day is flown, and you are sitting in a chilly room in San Francisco, and not on a wild crag in Scotland, or a glowing isle in the South Seas, or in the deepest icy caverns of the moon.

But the boy, the boy—what do I know of children, Colvin? I never had a brother or sister; I played alone and hardly had a friend until university years; I spent more time with my nurse Cummy than I ever did with neighborhood rascals, or close cousins, or schoolmates; indeed I spent more days out of school than in, being so sickly, and I doubt one in ten of my fellow scholars would remember my name, let alone a shared adventure. I have spent very little time with the children of my friends; I never taught or instructed a child in class or kirk; I have no issue of my own, and almost certainly never will, Fanny being forty years old. What do I know of children, who so recently was a child myself, deep into his twenties? Nothing: and the one shred of hope I have for my performance as a stepfather is that at least I have no experience to decry and disavow. It is all a clean slate for me, and there is just the one boy, after all—although I suspect that he is, as we all are, a hundred persons at once, depending on the hour, the weather, and the quality of his breakfast.

I must conclude here; I am away to the ferry to meet Fanny, in the city for dinner. I cover the pressing news quickly—the divorce is done, the deed to the cottage will be hers in a week, my financial situation is greatly righted by the letter from my father promising assistance, and my excellent and discerning friend Colvin will sell the enclosed pieces faster than a Scotsman can sing his favorite Burns air. In short order I will be married, Colvin—married! Me, of all the blessed men on earth! And no man was ever happier at the prospect, despite his secret fears about becoming husband and father all at once, bachelor to patriarch in a twinkling. I believe it will be a day in May, our wedding, probably at the cottage itself in Oakland; with all my heart I wish you could be there, though I know you and all our friends will be there in spirit, smiling broadly and reaching for the best of the wines. It will be a family affair, I suppose, with perhaps only Lloyd and his sister Isobel and her husband Joe in attendance, as the dashing Lieutenant Osbourne has not been invited; but I am of a mind to invite my two good friends here, my subtle landlady and her most interesting husband, with whom I spend many hours by the fire, hearing the most remarkable and unforgettable tales of his life and adventures. Was I the writer I so wish to be, I would devote a whole tremendous book to his adventures in various regions of the world, for no man I ever met has traveled so widely and well; but first I must finish the work I have before me, and then marry the woman I love, and after that we shall see what strange fate befalls the undersigned,

Who is ever your most appreciative
and thankful friend,
R.L.S.

"When last we spoke," said Mr Carson by the fire, "I was at sea, as it were, homeward from Australia, headed eventually to this very house, though I did not know that then; and while I may have mentioned that I was awhile among the

Sandwich Islands, it is another port that absorbs me this evening. Our ship made a number of landfalls—it was a trading vessel, and as I remember it stopped in Nouméa, Suva, Apia, and Rawaki, and even the recitation of those tropical names brings me back to those remote islets and atolls, so far from cities that you could well imagine you had never seen a building without a thatch, and always had walked in singing sand, under drifting birds of every color, never far from the seethe of surf.

"And then across the long empty continent of the North Pacific, day after day sliding through the gray seas; it was a stormy passage, to be sure, though it was a good ship, and a good crew, some of whom I see still, when they are in the city, looking for berths—good crews stick together beyond their time on the ship, you know, and often seek ships together, in twos and threes; and even occasionally a whole complement of men will sign onto a ship as a package, from mates down to the able-bodied and ordinary seamen. The two fellows who talked about Robert Emmet that night— they were mates of mine on that ship from Australia to Canada.

"Finally we arrived in Fort Victoria, which is on the tip of Vancouver Island. Now, I had been in Victoria here and there, and politely disliked its imperial hauteur, but I had never been up into the dense wilderness of the island itself, and a shipmate volunteered to steer me around, as he had friends in every little settlement and logging camp. Neither of us had a care in the world just then—we'd been paid off fair and honest, it was high summer, and we were fancy-free and curious. I had heard many stories about it; that it was the thickest jungle in North America, that there were otters and salmon there longer than the tallest man, that cougars were as common as street-cats, that the island had its own species of forest wolf, and that the people who had lived there for thousands of years were able to vanish as they liked, and turn themselves into birds in the blink of an eye, and talk to animals as if they had walked together from the womb.

"These were the Kwakwaka'wakw people, on the north end of the island, and it was among them we stayed a few weeks, after making our way up the inland coast of the island. What a trip that was, north to Kwakwaka'wakw country! Not once did it rain, not once did we encounter the slightest trouble, not once did we fail to find a meal when hunger shook us by the hand; it was like we were boys again, adventuring in the woods in summer, though both my friend and I were astounded by the sheer *size* of things there, so unlike our native cragland and rocky farms. Such trees as you could not even see their peaks; more eagles and fish-hawks than jaybirds and crows; and many times we surprised bears along the shore, for the bears there are excellent fisher-folk, and no tide pool is beyond their reach, that I noticed.

"But beyond my natural curiosity about this teeming wilderness, beyond my urge to explore new land and see new sights, was some other subtle thing, and I am at a loss even now to find words to explain or articulate that thing. I suppose it had something to do with the young sailor on the bench in Sydney Harbor; it was he who saw something in me that I had not perhaps admitted, though I think I always knew it—that I was absorbed and riveted by the girl from the stone village. I did not know her name, I knew nothing of her life, it was inconceivable that she would have escaped that lonely mountain, and found her way off the island, and across the sea, and across the terrific sprawl of this continent; but I tell you I felt some powerful and inchoate draw, some inarguable insistence, some magnetic force that I could not

resist, had I wanted to; but I had no thought of resistance, and went ever north, until I had come among the Kwakwa-ka'wakw.

"There are many stories I could tell of that time, for that is a riveting people, and there are many stories and legends about them; that their ancestors came to the island as fish and birds and bears and otters, and once home where they were meant to be, shucked their animal skins, and took the forms of people, though there were Kwakwaka'wakw people when I was there who could return as they liked to their ancestral shapes, and did so occasionally, as I more than once saw for myself. They were mostly fishers, and masterful at the craft, though they also knew every part and plant of their land that could produce food. As with any people there were great ones among them and craven ones, the gentle and the greedy, the generous and the prim; I knew a few to be thieves, and one to be a rapist, although he vanished when we were there, and while it was commonly said he had left the island, I suspect his spirit also left his body in that place, and his body returned to the ocean from whence his people came.

"They were no sort of noble savages, as some imagine wilderness people to be; they kidnapped and abused slaves, and they went to war, and they allowed layers of incomprehensible privilege in their society, just as we do in ours, whereby one man lords it over another for no discernible reason other than the accident of his parentage, or the riches left to him by genetic chance, or by the spurious claim that his ancestor was a small or large king, whatever that word means; and their men were as cruel and dismissive to their women as we are.

"But they were a great people also, capable of immense generosity and grace, as I often had occasion to see; the custom of theirs I admired most was the measure of greatness among them, that he who gave away the most was the best man; so that the men they admired the most were sometimes those who lived most like paupers, passing every sort of wealth quickly through their hands into the hands of those who needed it more. Hunters did this as a matter of course, as did those who gathered plants and berries; so that no one that I ever saw there went hungry, or was in need for long. I well remember a young man flush with the triumph of his first elk, coming around to every door to give away a prime cut of the meat. His name was Kwikw, the eagle, a remarkable young man who taught me much about his people and their place. I came to much affection for that boy, and came to think of him as a sort of nephew or young cousin, and we stay in touch, as much as possible, though he is not much for letters, and I am not often back in Kwakwaka'wakw country.

"Nor is he, now, for his people were decimated by disease, and even when I was there you could see them fading from the land. They were loath to leave, for they felt, understandably enough, and rightly, I think, that as soon as they left their place, they were no longer quite themselves, but shadows or ghosts, unrooted and uprooted. My shipmate, a perceptive man, said also that as soon as they left they would lose their land, for it would be stolen, one way or another, by

either business or government, if there is a difference between the two; and while he was right, that was not the first
concern of the Kwakwaka'wakw; they mourned the loss of
everything they knew in the most tactile and sensual way,
the scents and sounds, the way the mist slid in and out of the
firs, the wail of gulls, the sheen of seals, the melancholy
exhalation of whales sliding by under the terrific stars. The
clawing mud, the sift of sand, the scrabble of pebbles in the
surf; the plaint of owls, the scent of cedar, the bite of huckle-
berries from a certain thicket in a certain season—they were
convinced that these things were part and parcel of their
being, and who is to gainsay them? I think there are many
more true things than we know, or will ever know, and the
wisest man among us is the one who is first to say 'I do not
know, and will never know, and everything I do know is one
pebble among the uncountable pebbles wrought by the sea.'"

He paused, for a while, and then smiled, and apologized
for waxing philosophical, which is one of the lesser vices,
and a habit that Mrs Carson, bless her perspicacity, said he
would be wise to break; he was trying assiduously, he said,
to only wax philosophical on Tuesdays, and so reduce the
sin to a weekly thing, like whiskey or cigars, best enjoyed
in parsimonious dosages.

He paused again, lost in thought; I remember the flicker
of the fire on his face, and the color of his eyes, a sort of gray
and green at once, like the sea. Then he said, "Mr Stevenson,
have I ever told you how I came by this mark on my neck?
It is a falcon, and it was placed there by my young friend

Kwikw, because one day I told him how I had been drawn to his country by a feeling I could not explain or understand, a feeling so powerful I could not actively resist it, though it made no sense by the measure of the world. I had savored my time in the dense wet wilderness of his country, and counted him as a new friend, and stored up my experience of a proud people that I would always remember and mostly admire, except for their constant yearning for the days when they sold and traded and herded other human beings, treating them worse than they did their pet animals. But I felt my time in the north to be coming to an end, and I felt that I had missed something, that something had gone undone, or unrealized; and I did not know what that thing was.

"He listened with great attention, Kwikw; he was, and is, a remarkable young man, capable of much beyond the reach of words and intellect, I think; and then he went away for three days, on a fishing trip into the rich straits northeast of the island. My shipmate and I prepared to leave, and head back to San Francisco to find a ship; we thought we might travel through Seattle and Portland, to see the new towns where it was said that the residents swam through hip-deep mud, or rode immense timbers, and spoke dialects they had learned from the red-haired people who had lived there for thousands of years.

"We were ready to set out, one morning, when Kwikw returned, and asked me to come with him to the shore. Down we went, through the halls of the huge old trees, to a little shingle of beach he knew, a place of power, he said, where the falcons nested in the cliffs and great bears came for reasons of their own. He took me knee-deep into the sea and explained that he was going to sew a falcon into my skin, just below my ear, because he had been given a message, and the falcon wanted to travel with me the rest of my days, would I permit that? Now, I was a man of the sea, and knew many a man covered with ink and markings, though it was never something that appealed to me, but I trusted Kwikw, and he spoke so fervently from the heart that I could not say no; so he marked me, as you see. When he was finished he also marked my eyes and mouth and ears with sea water, a sort of baptism, as religious people would say, and then we walked back up onto the pebbled beach.

"To my surprise there was a man waiting for us there, by the path down which we had come through the forest—a man as grizzled and covered with fur as if he was a bear himself. Not a big man, but something about him was strong; you had the instant and inarguable feeling that he was not a man to fight. It seemed to me he was not Kwakwaka'wakw, although you could hardly make out his face for all the hair and fur—so much that you could not tell where his beard ended and his coat began. He and Kwikw talked quietly for a moment, and then Kwikw said to me that this man would take me where I should go, and that I should accompany him, and trust him implicitly, no matter what the circumstances in which I found myself. The man then approached me, and examined the falcon on my neck, without a word to me; and then he indicated that I should follow him into the forest, which I did."

Just then Mrs Carson spoke gently from the kitchen door, saying that dinner was ready; I had been so immersed in the scene on the pebbly beach that I had not heard her footstep, and I startled at her voice. Mr Carson smiled and rose from his chair, murmuring of roast oysters, but I could not refrain from asking him about the furred man—was he . . . ?

"His name is Gérard Harrison," said Mr Carson, "and his story is one that Mrs Carson must tell you, for she knows him far better than I do, though I have the greatest esteem for him. I suggest you catch Mrs Carson sometime when she has an hour to spare, and ask her about Gérard; and you will hear a tale that not even the greatest novelist could invent, for its twists and turns and mysteries. Ah, it *is* roasted oysters! Is there a more alluring scent in the world than that to a hungry man? Let us get to the table before the rest of the house leaves us nothing but dry shells. Shall we?"

*

I have been at pains in this account to be as accurate as I can, with the soaring stories and rhythms of speech I heard in Mrs Carson's house, during my months there; but I am well aware that this is not the sort of book many readers want—*it is a tide of competing voices, is all it is!*, I hear the disconsolate reviewers say, who so wished for headlong adventure, and a narrative arc, and dark villains vanquished, and tumultuous hearts, and mysterious heroes and heroines slowly becoming aware of their deeper selves, slowly becoming more self-aware—slowly, perhaps, maturing. And what of love stories, a staple of our literature, rightly so? The love stories in this account are already launched, and where is our desperate fellow yearning for a woman who loves another, or our innocent girl pining for a preening cad, or the good woman gone bad by virtue of her own inflexible ego? Are we to read all the way through these pages, and find nothing but the brave and courteous Mr Carson, and the gentle and remarkable Mrs Carson, and the idyllic Fanny Osbourne across the bay, and her young and callow lover, all of them with good manners and the best intentions? Have we no evil and illness with which to contend, no horror and conflict in which to happily be aghast, in that evening hour when we read by the fire, or sprawl in bed beneath the sputtering night-light?

Trust me, I feel as you do; and this is all the more ironic, for *I* dream daily and nightly of the books I want so fervently to write, filled with headlong escapes across Highland meadows, and ferocious battles on remote islands, and terrifying chases and hauntings on icy moors, and spirits emerging from fantastic bottles, and black-hearted nobles outwitted by noble woodsmen whose arrows unerringly find their targets. No one loves a dashing tale more than I do, and O!, how I yearn to write one after another, as fast as I can get the words from my pen, and shiver and delight readers of every age from nine to ninety! And I *will,* too—I will, if He who spoke the stars alight grants me ten more years, or twenty. Surely no more than that, for many times I have already thought I had coughed my last, and the most optimistic soul, staring at the grinning skeleton I have become, would place no sensible bet on many more years for me in this world. But give me ten, Lord, give me twenty, and I swear I will write such books as will never be forgotten, books that roar and sing and chime and ring, books that children hide under their mattresses to read secretly after the house is asleep, books that judges and priests keep in their innermost sanctums to pore over, while ostensibly studying the scriptures of their crafts! Books to thrill children and entrance men and women, books that cry out to be set on the stage, books that will never go out of print, for there will always be those who seek them out to remember that first thrill, and those who stumble over them in bookshops and libraries and the dens of friends, and open them curiously, and are whirled away by a tropical scent, the clash of swords, the crash of surf, the rattle of faraway hooves in the night.

But I cannot make this account into that sort of wonderful novel; for I wish most of all to capture something of what *is,* right here around me, right now, in this house, and I could not bear to invent a jot of it—sometimes it *is* a sin to invent, when the real tale is there to be told; and here are two people of rare grace and generosity, whose lives are more amazing than the most outlandish novels, who spent years traveling toward each other, knowing somehow and not knowing at all their final destination in each other's hearts; and I alone am given to tell thee of them, having entered their home by utter chance, and been graced to discover not merely landlady and husband, but two riveting friends, two rare adventurers, two gentle lovers whose slightest glance at each other, I can report, having seen it many times, is filled with such mutual affection and wonder, that you would think they married yesterday, and not a year ago come May.

March 9, 1880, Oakland, California

Dear Louis,

Mother says I can call you Louis in my letter because soon we are to be related and related people use first names. I have two first names as you know and while everyone calls me Sam I like that *you* call me Lloyd. I would like to be Lloyd now. My father is Sam and I am not him. You called me Lloyd right from the beginning which I like very much. I would like to go sailing as much as we can when you marry Mother. She says we can go by ourselves if we want. I would like that. Perhaps we can sail to Sausalito. Mother says we will go to Scotland after you are married. If everyone in Scotland is like you that is a thin country (joke). Isobel and Joe Strong come by once a week for dinner. Joe says he will fix the broken things in the house but he does not get around to it. Isobel is happy you are marrying Mother. She says it is long past time Mother is appreciated for who she really is a wonderful mysterious woman. She says you understand Mother more than anyone else ever. She says she only hopes you don't cough yourself to death before the wedding (joke). Joe Strong says he will do a sweet of paintings on your wedding day but I don't think he will get around to it. I would like to fish for sturgeon also if we can sometime. Mother says your friend John Carson knows boats and he can perhaps find us a boat or take us fishing. I saw a sturgeon last week displayed at the fish shop and it was so big it hung over the table at both ends. The shopman said it was fifty feet long but I think he was exasperating about the size. I cannot wait until you live here with us. I am ready to change schools as you and Mother think best. I am excited for Scotland but worried I do not speak any Scotlish. Isobel is happy with Joe but I think she worries like Mother did with my father. Mother does not worry like that with you. Please come visit soon and bring the boat. Remember my name is Lloyd now. You will have to remind Mother who calls me Sam and sometimes when she does that she stops and gets that look on her face that you and I talked about (secret). Mother says to tell you that the lilacs look ready to bloom and the buckbrush *did* bloom and she planted lilies and asters and has the highest hope for both. She does not have the highest hopes for the shooting stars. Yesterday a deer ate the pea plants but left the monkey-flowers alone. I thought you should know. Write me right back if you can. The postman says your letters are his favorites because of the drawings on the envelopes. His name is Mason but he is not a mason (joke).

Yrs most sincerely
S. Lloyd Osbourne

As I have said before, boarders flowed in and out of the house so steadily that as soon as I recognized a face, chances were excellent it was gone forever the next day, with naught to remember its owner by, than a glove or a hat or a pair of forgotten boots; but as my own tenure in the house grew longer so did my attentiveness to my fellow passengers in the tall wooden vessel, and I recount some of those souls now,

partly from sheer wonder at the variety of life, but also now with a novelist's deeper appreciation of the fact that any ten minutes with any being on earth could produce ten novels, had you the perception and imagination to see the stories waiting anxiously to be told.

So then, let us begin with some of the women I met in the house. Not residents, I hasten to add—Mrs Carson ran a respectable domicile—but women who passed through the doors as friends and family of residents, assistants to Mrs Carson about the house, and friends and acquaintances of Mr and Mrs Carson. Let me start with the latter, for two in particular stay in my memory.

One was a woman who was the unsung chess champion of her native country; that is to say it was she who trained, advised, and directed the nominal champion, her husband, who, according to Mr Carson, found this arrangement intimately romantic, and refused to play or travel unless her travel expenses were covered also. She was, according to Mr Carson, a person of the most wonderfully infinitesimal ego; he had met her through her brother, one of his many shipmates, later lost at sea. It was the late brother, said Mr Carson, who had invented a system of signals whereby she might direct her husband during a match, each action or inaction on her part indicating the piece in which he ought to focus his full and fervid attention—she would sigh, stretch, run a hand through her hair, adjust her dress, fiddle with a button, or remain stock-still when he glanced in her direction, and then leave it to him to see what nefarious plot or subtle opening she had seen and would suggest he defend or exploit. "To give him his due," said Mr Carson, "he rarely *does* look over at her, and he has played many a match without doing so at all, and between you and me I believe it is the fact of her presence that acts as a boon to him, more than any hint of direction; but once when I suggested this to her, she replied that in all the matches they had played together privately, he had never once beaten her; and that, I say with admiration, is the one and only time I have ever heard her express even a jot of ego; although it is an interesting distinction, if there is one, between ego and pride, and perhaps it was more of an expression of quite justifiable pride in a very rare skill."

The other was a woman who had, said Mrs Carson quietly, established a flourishing house of ill repute, in Sacramento, and then had a crisis of conscience, and converted each and every one of her employees to other lines of work, with a remarkable diligence. This was a Mrs Adams, a formidable woman with whom I spent an hour by the fire one cold and foggy morning, and I think I shall always account that hour one of my best spent, for she was a wry and witty woman with no illusions whatsoever about social mores, and every firm conviction about honest right and wrong. "It was wrong of me," she said, "to profit by sexual activity, and right of me to atone by investing all that profit and more into other activities," she said. "I hold no truck with religions and their fear of sex, and I cannot bear pompous edicts issued by one soul about the sexual activities of another, but I also could not continue to profit myself by the sexual labor of others, for that is what it becomes, a terrible labor, a cruel slavery, a mean and evil twist of the zest of sex, a gift that should never be sold or bent to other purposes than its design, which is a wonderfully intimate and private pleasure between lovers. It seemed to me finally that I was robbing and enslaving women by pandering to the worst impulses of men, who did not at all wish intimacy, but only their own brief pleasure; and that realization, as well as an epiphany one night, that each girl in my employ was in a very real way my own child, was enough to change my course on a permanent basis." One of her former employees, she said, had become a detective, one was in Burma in the court of Queen Supayalat, several were teachers, one had become an expert in cordage, and several, after consulting with Mrs Carson, were involved in the buying and selling of properties in and around San Francisco. One was a noted painter of portraits, one had entered religious orders, and one had become a journalist specializing in crimes committed by the upper classes.

Mrs Carson, as I may have mentioned, also seemed to have a fairly regular rotation of girls from her native Ireland passing through the house, generally for a month at a time, as far as I could tell, and apparently always two by two; in my four months at Bush Street there were eight young women who assisted Mrs Carson with the endless duties of the house, and I recount them two by two, as I met and remember them. There were Alice and Loretta, who refused to even look at each other, let alone speak civilly, though they worked together all day; reportedly the root of their mutual dislike was a young man in Belfast. There were Mairead and Fiona, both from County Mayo, and both slim as saplings. There were Brigid and Deidre, both from Wicklow, they told me, and Deidre from a forest so deep that no one had ever successfully mapped it; Deidre was of the opinion that the forest did not *want* to be mapped, and so changed form at will to confound surveyors and land agents. "Indeed, sir," she said, "there's men who went into it and never came back out, and are entombed in the trees, men who would have done the woods harm, and the woods would not suffer it, and so took them away into itself, and there are many more stories like this that I have heard."

And there were Ailís and her friend Éadaoin, the latter at pains to instruct me that her name in the Irish meant "joyous friend," which she was, of Ailís, the two of them having been best friends since they were three years old. They had come to America together, "a tale you could tell for years and never arrive at even the middle of it," said Ailís, mysteriously. I remember those two young women particularly for their singing—they sang all day at their work, most beautifully, in their native tongue, with an apparently inexhaustible supply of songs, for never that I recall did I hear the same song twice. Also I remember that once when a singing teacher stayed a week in the house, he tried with all his might to teach Éadaoin the American song "Shenandoah," but when she began to sing it for the house one night, out of her mouth came the most horrendous caterwauling, at which she rushed downstairs to her room in tears; Ailís said quietly that their voices only knew Irish, and refused to sing in another language, and that the singing teacher ought to be ashamed of himself, for mortifying Éadaoin's voice that way—"it will be a week before her voice comes back all shy and fearful, and we will have to coax the poor thing back up into her mouth again; they're terrible shy, voices are, skittery as wrens in a wind."

★

One morning I came down to the kitchen early for coffee and found Mrs Carson preparing to voyage up Pine Street to Octavia, where she knew a man who sold the freshest most succulent oysters in all the bay, but only once every few weeks, when circumstances arranged themselves to allow a shipment; a few people only knew of this resource, as the oysterman would sell only to people he admired and trusted, of whom Mrs Carson was one. The seller was in the habit, Mrs Carson said, of hoisting a signal flag from the peak of his house on Octavia when there were oysters to be had, and as the signal had just been spotted by Éadaoin, as she worked on the top floor, she, Mrs Carson, was on the march. I offered to accompany her, to which she acquiesced politely, and off we went; and so arrived the hour for me to ask her finally about her friend Gérard Harrison, the bear hunter who wore a claw around his neck. I had not forgotten the way she startled and smiled when she had heard of him from Captain Smith; and I remembered too John Carson's grave respect both for the man and the story of how he had been of assistance to Mrs Carson, a story Mr Carson would not tell, as it was so valuable and crucial for her.

Up Pine Street we went then, as it rose toward Nob Hill, and crested at Mason, and declined to the west at Leavenworth, and rose again finally to our destination on Octavia; and I will ask the reader to imagine for herself or himself the crystalline morning, one of those middle-March days in San Francisco when the sky is a remarkable and cloudless cerulean blue, and the wind is only the most occasional redolent caress, and the air is filled with the spice of eucalyptus and madrone, sifted here and there with tendrils of lime and lemon; behind us the glittering bay, ahead the prospect of a glimpse of mother sea; and all along our way houses and buildings of every sort of wood and iron and stone, piled and jumbled and shouldered together like rugby players in pursuit of their beloved and slippery ball.

It was as Pine Street rose gently at Kearny that I asked after the bear hunter, and Mrs Carson smiled and said that she would endeavor to tell me the first half of the story uphill, and the second half downhill, and if she shaped the tale right, we would finish at 680 Bush Street, for Mr Harrison was, in a real sense, responsible for her residence there.

For a moment she was silent, as we climbed, and then she brought me back to the small irascible man in Montreal—the tiny man she thought to be *soilsithe,* one of the illuminated beings—the door-porter at the school, who welcomed her and fed her, on the first day she was on this continent, frightened and cold and starving. A tidal moment, she reminded me; and then there was another, she said; "equally unlooked for, equally momentous as the first word of a long story, a story still telling me, as it were. . . ."

She had spent the day sleeping in an attic room at the school, the students all being away, and when she came downstairs again at dusk to the kitchen, she found the tiny man in conversation with a man as furred and hairy, you would almost say, as a bear. This was Mr Harrison, she discovered, and he had somehow been summoned by the tiny man, and tasked with escorting her on her journey across Canada; Mr Harrison was adept and familiar with the wilderness, and no better guide could be found in the whole country, nor one more trustworthy as a companion; it turned out that Mr Harrison too had once come to the tiny man for guidance and intercession, at a terribly low point in his life, and he too had been relieved of his burden through the testy intercession of the little porter, and had then in gratitude sworn service to him in whatever capacity, whenever that service was required.

"I was startled," said Mrs Carson, "at the idea of a journey across Canada; I had said nothing of such an endeavor, nor even imagined such a thing; but here it was all planned out, and Mr Harrison eager to be away at once, and the tiny man pressing money into my hand, with a look of disgruntled impatience that I remember yet. I stammered, I began to protest; but the porter said, with the oddest sort of rude tenderness, that he was only an intermediary in these things, and that he was in a great hurry to get back to his work, and I should take it from him as inarguable fact that I was headed west, as far west as I could go in this land, and that I was utterly meant to do so, and had been headed in that direction since the morning I met the man on the mountain, and that tiny man had seen this meeting clear as day, not once but several times before my arrival, and once since as a confirmatory message, and he had been instructed inarguably as to what it meant, and I had been delivered to him alone, of all people in Canada, so that he could be of service, which he was attempting to deliver, and that Mr Harrison was himself the service, and that I was egregiously wasting his time and Mr Harrison's and my own with this hesitant hemming and hawing, and that the sooner we were through his door the better, because his door would quite soon be hammered upon by yet another person who wrongly expected him to accomplish anything at all except by abashed intercession unto those whose feet he was not worthy to wash.

"All the time he was saying these words he was edging me quite rudely toward the door, and just as he said the word 'wash' he pushed me abruptly into the hallway, where stood Mr Harrison silent and smiling, and then he slammed the door, with a loud crash, and that was the last time I ever saw him—to this day when I hear a door slam I think of him, and feel the most complicated rush of emotions. I doubt there is a more intemperate man in all of Canada, a ruder man, a testier man, a more truculent and disputatious man; yet he is an extraordinary man, a man whose whole life and work has been in service to people he does not know and never sees twice, for the most part. In one way he is a slave and another way a man rich beyond our understanding and imagination."

And just as she said this, we achieved Octavia Boulevard, and she went to conduct her business, while I waited, pondering her story. That a man can be two men at once, or four, or forty, this I know, too well, I suppose, for I was myself many men as a youth, trying on selves one after another, sometimes through the eyes and arms of others, too; and more than once I was one man one moment and another man altogether the next; so much so that sometimes I lost the actual man for days at a time, and wandered selfless, as it were. I grew up, I shucked selves, I learned to be one man only, and let him be liked or not as the world wished; and for me Fanny's love was the final blow to my other selves, for she loved the real man, and has no time or truck with the others, and so, starved of attention, they have fled, and I only am escaped alone to tell thee, as the messenger says to Job, in the Book of Books.

Walking downhill in San Francisco is an art—it is a controlled fall, more than any sort of orthodox perambulation. You fall slowly, scurrying to keep your legs under you; you lean forward with one part of your body and lean backward with the rest; you must consciously resist the urge to simply surrender to the lure of gravity, and roll headlong down the street, until you eventually plop into one body of water or another; and all this becomes unconscious, the longer you live there, so eventually you hardly notice the peaks and valleys, the laborious up and skittering down, and only at night can you gauge the nature of your walks, by the particular ache of your legs—if your calves complain, you have been going uphill all day, and if your thighs protest, it has been all downhill; and it is the curious nature of this most rippling of cities that it is either one or another, and never both. You would think that the miles climbed up would be equal to the miles skipped down, but not in San Francisco; indeed there are stories of men here who have done nothing but

climb uphill their entire lives, and so outdone the most famous alpinists, who only climb one mountain at a time,
where San Franciscans climb a dozen a day, while chatting
of this and that, and the price of coal.

Down Bush Street we went now, blessed with oysters—
the long slow swell and sweep of Bush Street, from its peak
south of the old Presidio fort, down to where it ends at the
bay, and sometimes *in* it—I have seen barrels and casks roll
rattling from the street and plop into the bay, followed by
shouting men and laughing boys, and wondered sometimes
if the bay does not somehow exact tribute from the city, and
require a daily tot of wine and beer, delivered by nominal
accident, each street taxed according to its volume of traffic.

On our way back down the hill I asked Mrs Carson about
her voyage across Canada with Mr Harrison, but she had
grown somewhat reticent, and would only say that it was a
long while in the traveling. She fell silent for a moment, and
I wondered if I would ever hear the last part of her story; but
then she said quietly that sometimes even now she dreamed
of that journey, dreamed that she was once again walking
and canoeing and riding boats and trains and wagons, and
when she awoke she was actively startled to find herself in a
bed, in a room, in a house, with a husband she loved dearly,
in a city, and not high in the mountains on wintry trails, or
jostling across the sprawling plains of Saskatchewan and
Manitoba in a battered old wagon, with Mr Harrison taciturn beside her.

"I suppose Canada to me will always be partly a dream,"

she said, as we crossed Polk Street. "I was often weary, and sometimes ill, and what I remember best is plodding along behind Mr Harrison. He was not much for talk then and there were days at a time when he said not a word. In the first weeks of our journey I did my best to elicit from him his relationship to our Montreal friend, and how they had come to have such close dealings, and where we might be headed, and something, anything, of his own life; but not until we reached the mountains of Alberta did he seem to relax. Later he told me he disliked and distrusted flat land, 'oppressed land,' as he called it; it was a fixed idea of his that flat open land was dangerous, there being no place to hide, and 'no place never trod upon,' as he said. Whereas the mountains and forests, or so he thought, were endlessly mysterious, and never would be fully explored or enslaved to do the work of man; just as soon as you have mapped them, and set out your trails, and marked what is where, the woods pays no attention to you and your puny map, and shifts things here and there as it pleases, and moves its creeks and rivers, and fills in your trails with its relentless green hands, and there's not much you can do about it, except cut down all the forests, which someday might well happen, as there's people would do such a thing, unthinkable evil though it be.

"This was how he talked," said Mrs Carson, as we crossed Jones Street, "sort of biblical and pantheist and free-form imaginative all at once, and he grew ever more talkative and even garrulous as we got deeper into the forest of British Columbia, headed always west to the sea. Late one night he told me that we were headed finally to Vancouver Island, to a place he knew that had power, as he said, and that him bringing me there was the payment of a debt, as it were, too complicated to explain; but that when I got to that place, a thing would be concluded that entailed several people's threads coming together. 'Putting the threads together is the work,' he said, an explanation that I still do not understand, though it is unlikely I will ever forget the phrase.

"Also the deeper we went into the woods the faster and thicker his hair and beard grew," said Mrs Carson, "which sounds preposterous, but I did witness this curious fact; so that by the time we came to the coast finally, my companion looked more like a bear than a man, though no one else we met remarked this at all, which I found curious. At a place called Broughton Island there were two young men waiting with a boat, though how they had known where to be and why was a mystery. They ferried us across to the bigger island, and after quite a long walk I found myself on a little rocky beach huddled between vast cliffs and pillars of rock.

"To my astonishment, Mr Harrison sat down here, and announced that we had arrived where we were headed, and that his task was done, and then, to my amazement, he leapt up and actually capered and danced on the beach! I confess I laughed aloud—you never saw a rougher man in your life, and I had seen him many times grim and threatening and rough to those he thought would harm or hinder us, on our journey across the country. But here he was, the famous hunter, the fearless mountain man, jigging and giggling like a child; indeed he whirled so haphazardly that he fell down in the surf, and crawled back up onto the beach dripping and laughing.

"I quizzed him as to what I was to do here in the wilderness, certainly I did, but he had no answer, and kept repeating that I would know when I knew, and that his task had been to get me here, and what happened after that was none of his business and not in his sack of knowledge, as he said; but then he grew thoughtful, and said, Now, miss, I see that you have to write the message, you have to write it with whatever tools are to hand, that be why you are in this place, miss, and he waved his hands at all the uncountable rocks and pebbles on the beach. I was taken aback, but now he was sure of himself, and his merriment bubbled back up again as he kept talking incomprehensibly about the message, the message.

"Finally he told me to gather as many small stones as I could carry, and bring them to a clearing at the head of the beach, and he would do the same, and this we did, again and again, so that there were thousands of stones there, a cairn as tall as me. I think I will always remember that little clearing—it was tucked out of the wind, and lined by trees and ferns in a perfect circle, and the floor of it was sand. I suppose it was an accident of geology, but it felt very much like a refuge, a place of peace, that the forest and the sea had agreed to leave between them, for mysterious reasons.

"Mr Harrison had now regained his usual calm, and he

said that I had best set to work, and that he had to go conduct a little business, but that I would be safe, and he would not be far away, but that I ought to get to work on the message, for the time had come. I was flummoxed, and tired, and I suppose a part of me was frightened too, for I was somewhat rude, and taxed him with mysterious muddle, and what could he possibly mean about a message? What message was I to write, and to whom?

"He stood there thinking for a moment—I can see him yet, with his beard bristling out from his face like a small animal, and the salt water still dripping from parts of his body—and then he said that he would ask me a question, and then he would go about his business, and I should think hard about the answer, and then write the message, and when I was done he would know, and he would come back. And his question was: where is your home?

"And with that he was gone," said Mrs Carson, "and you can imagine, from what I have told you about his woods craft, that when he wished to vanish, vanish he did, instantly and silently. I stood there awhile annoyed, and then I began to think, where *was* my home? What *was* home for me who had lost my family, my country, even my name? For when I lived in the stone village, no one spoke to me for a year at a time, no one called my name, no one had the word that meant me in their mouths, and there were long periods then when I had no word for me either.

"The village, the stone village, the empty stone huts, the wind-whipped mountain; that was my home, and that is what I built in the clearing. Even now I am amazed that I did that, but I did, first slowly, trying to remember which hut was where, and which were half-destroyed, and then faster and faster, my hands surer with the stones, whole lines of huts coming to life in minutes; and fastest and surest of all I built my own little hut, in which I had lived when I was no one, just a girl on a mountain, unremembered, unknown, unmourned, a child without a name.

"It was a frenzy, an ecstasy; as Mr Carson says, sometimes we do what must be done without knowing at all why we do so. And just as I finished I heard Gérard returning; but now there was someone with him. I jumped up and would have fled, I think, except that just then the two men came into the clearing, and stopped with surprise when they saw the stone village. As they stared at it I stared too, and it was as if I had new eyes, for now I could see how intricate and faithful it was, the entire tiny village of Sliabh Mór rebuilt exactly in miniature in a clearing in Canada, by another ocean on another side of the world.

"Gérard said nothing, although he was smiling so that I thought he would begin capering again, and the other man said nothing for a moment, as he stared at the stones; and then he slowly looked up, and . . . why, Mr Stevenson, here we are at home! And I have been prattling away, without the slightest consideration for your time and your work!"

"No, no, Mrs Carson," I said, still completely caught up in the story, "my work can wait—the man, Mrs Carson, the man! Who was the man?"

And just then, as if we were in a theatrical production, in a scene designed to draw gasps from the audience, the door to 680 Bush Street swung open, and there was Mr Carson smiling at us. I cannot remember if I gasped, but I do remember that a shiver ran up my spine, as I realized that, amazingly and unbelievably, that was how Mary and John had met again, twenty years after meeting each other for the first time at the door of the hut on Sliabh Mór.

March 30, 1880, Oakland, California

Dear Louis,

I will be brief—I have a moment to snatch from this and that, Isobel and Joe are here, and Lloyd has a terrible cold which worries me—I just wanted to say that I yearn for you—I crave your kiss and your hands on my skin and your eyes like coals burning into me—and your laugh, your quip, your banter—I *crave* it, I say, and I use the word deliberately. So long have I been a desert and you make me bloom. So long have I huddled around my children, an adamant wall between them and their wastrel father, and the travails that followed him like vultures, that I became a wall myself, and never knew it—and I would have stayed that way all my life, Louis, but for you—but for you sweeping into that hotel in France, and bowing, and staring at me with those merry eyes—O, Louis, never leave me, never betray me, never never never! I could not bear it, you know—I couldn't. Everything that is good in me still

reaches for you and yearns for you and drinks you in
like light and water granted an old gnarled tree that
never thought to blossom again; but I am blossoming, I
feel it every hour, every day, I grow and laugh and
Lloyd asks me if I feel well, for he has not seen me so
lighthearted and free in his whole life, poor lamb. He is
calling and I must go and I tell you every day that passes
without you in it is an eternity—but one day closer to
the day we shall be married and after that never parted
not for a day or a night—that we found each other is a
miracle, my love, a miracle! All my kisses and tears,

> *Your loving*
> *Fanny*

It was Mr Carson who told me the rest of the story—by the
fire, of course, this time after an oyster supper; and we had a
bottle of fine wine between us, and for once his story did
not end magically an instant or two before Mrs Carson called
us in to dine, and I was not left hanging, and I did not conclude that night that he was a master of timing and pace in
storytelling, gauging each segment of his story to a fine point,
so as to leave me thirsty for it on a nightly basis. No, for once
he was expansive, and the story stretched and wandered like
a river, always forward, but happy to eddy and slack, as well
as rapid and pool; and even now, long after that evening, I
remember it with deep affection, as well as sadness; for it was,
in a sense, the last night, the final chapter, the end of a time
I had come to love. I think I did not know until that eve-

ning how deeply I had come to like Mr and Mrs Carson; in part because that evening was when I knew my time with them was coming to an end. Always it is thus, I suppose, that the sharpest savor is the last, and we finally understand what we have, when we no longer have it. A deep delight, married to a deep throb of sadness—perhaps that is the quintessential human condition.

His voice grainy and amused in the flicker of the firelight; the excellent wine vanishing gently in our glinting glasses; his story moving from the clearing to a boat, and to Vancouver city, and eventually to San Francisco; his tone warm and reverential as he spoke of her courage, her many adventures in Ireland after he had met her that morning by the hut— "whole volumes and *sets* of volumes might be written, Mr Stevenson, whole *shelves* about her travels, her companions, her enemies, her escapes and rescues, her endurance, her visions and times of darkness, her travails and her subtlety, what she lost and what she gained; she is a remarkable soul, a woman of parts, one whose passage through the freighted air creates ripples that do not subside, I think; but those are her stories to tell, to shape and share as she likes; and you will be a lucky man if you hear a hundredth of them. . . ."

How they stepped off a ship at Mission Street Wharf, and walked hand-in-hand through the city, marveling at its scents and breezes, the billow of its topography, the dozens of languages, the welter of voices, the crisp bronze light unlike that in any city they had ever seen; how they rode to Blue Mountain, the highest point in the city, and there promised themselves to each other, for every day of the rest of their lives, with the hope of going together into whatever is next after death; how they knocked at 680 Bush Street, and met a friend of Mr Harrison's, who was eager to sell the house, and more eager still to sell it in such a way that he was free to vanish from the city, off to Alaska, with payments made not to him but to many citizens young and old over the course of many years, according to an intricate plan which he entrusted to Mrs Carson, in whom he reposed complete faith; how they were married at Notre Dame des Victoires on Bush Street, their wedding celebrated by Mr Carson's companion from the war, and guests coming from far and wide, guests from several nations speaking several languages, all united in esteem and joy; and how their first wedding anniversary was approaching, on the second day of May, and he, Mr Carson, had hatched a conspiracy for two, which entailed a picnic on Blue Mountain, at the very spot where troth had been plighted, with the most savory oysters in California, and wines from a vineyard in Napa that he particularly respected and recommended to me if and when I was planning a honeymoon after my own wedding; and just when, Mr Stevenson, *is* your wedding?

Answer: sometime in May, probably around the ides, when all financial and legal matters were settled, Lloyd released from school, and the weather bucolic. Fanny was of the opinion that we should be married at the cottage in Oakland, in the yard, amid a crush of May flowers, so that we could begin our married life together in the free air and bright sun, beneath no stern ceiling or authoritative roof, confined by no chapel or church, joined finally to each other by each other, with hearts as open as the wedding venue; but for once I could not agree with her, for while I admired her impulse and agreed wholeheartedly with her vision, I wanted nothing whatsoever of Lieutenant Samuel Osbourne in the air that day—not his name, not his former presence, not the fact that the property on which we would stand had once been his. Nor, I found, did I want to be married in Oakland, after my residence in San Francisco; something in me loved this old salty city, and wanted to begin my marital voyage here, in this port, and in no other. Something of the city's music and flavor, its character and characters, its scents and sounds, its bones and sinews, had become a part of me, in ways I could not explain, though my profession be tacking sentences to emotions, as a man papers a wordless wall with garrulous handbills.

Fanny was not pleased, I will report, but her mind is quick and deep, and she realized the depth of my feeling, though I could not articulate it; and so she arranged for us to be married on Post Street, at the home of a minister, the Reverend Doctor Scott, a wry gentleman with a beard like an Icelandic epic, endless and prickly with detail. Her friend Dora Williams, wife of the painter Virgil Williams, would attend her, and I would stand alone, as the two men I might have chosen as my best men were both across the Atlantic,

Sidney Colvin in England and my cousin Bob Stevenson in Scotland; I thought for a moment of asking Fanny's son Lloyd to stand with me, but he was so young, and hard enough for him to watch his mother marry, that I determined to stand alone.

But of course I did not stand alone, on the day; and there is a story in who it was who stood by me as best man and witness. Of course there is a story. There is a story in every thing, and every being, and every moment, were we alert to catch it, were we ready with our tender nets; indeed there are a hundred, a thousand stories, uncountable stories, could they only be lured out and appreciated; and more and more now I realize that what I thought was a skill only for authors and pastors and doctors and dream-diviners is the greatest of all human skills, the one that allows us into the heart and soul and deepest layers of our companions on the brief sunlit road between great dark wildernesses. We are here to witness, to apprehend, to see and hear, to plumb, with patience and humility, the shy stories of others; and in some cases, like mine, then shape and share them; so that they might sometimes, like inky arrows, sink into the depths of other men and women and children, and cause pleasure, or empathy, or a sort of delicious pain, as you realize that someone somewhere else, even perhaps in a time long ago, felt just as you did. Stories, among their many virtues, are messages from friends you did not know you had; and while you may well never meet the friend, you feel the better, with one more companion by your side, than you thought you knew.

April 14, 1880, 680 Bush Street, San Francisco

My dear Colvin,

The briefest of notes to convey the greatest of news;
I am finally, happily, thoroughly, astoundingly, to be
married, on May 19, in this lovely city by the sea, to the
lovely Miss Frances, who is now free of her previous
marital tumult and prison, and willingly accepts my
proposal of marriage, and consents to accept me in holy
wedlock, to be joined thereunto by a cheerful and
jocular Reverend Scott, whom I have met, and whom, I
report with peals of laughter, said to me "Stevenson?
Now I have read the essays of a young R. L. *Stevenson* of
Edinburgh," specifically *On Falling in Love,* and *Crabbed
Age and Youth,* and *An Apology for Idlers,* and *Child's Play,*
and *Walking Tours,* and *A Plea for Gas Lamps,* and my
study of Rabbie Burns, which he told me, in all seriousness,
he collectively found arch, and mannered, and somewhat *brittle* with self-consciousness, though he had the
inchoate idea, he confided, that this young fellow *might,*
just might, you understand, with some seasoning and
experience, become a decent essayist, could he learn to
not be quite so *aware* of himself, but just blurt down
thought and feeling on the page, without undue
consideration of the product until *after* it had been
allowed to emerge from the heart, without detour
through the head. He told me this with such genuine
generosity of spirit, such unadorned respect for literature
and its possibilities, such compassion for poor young

Mr R. L. Stevenson of Edinburgh and his overartful capering, that I hesitated long to tell him who I was; but you cannot ask a reverend minister to celebrate your marriage without admitting your name. I informed him gently that I was that very man, young Mr R. L. Stevenson of Edinburgh, the larval essayist, and you should have seen his face, Colvin! Such a rapid series of expressions, such a swift and humorous parade of emotions written as clear as day! But again to his credit, for he seems a most wonderfully honest and forthright soul, he apologized with a great shout of laughter, and called himself names, and hoped that I would glean a nugget of use amid the flood of his foolishness, and then we went over the order of service with Fanny. A most interesting and entertaining man, and I will take to heart what he had to say about a certain author's brittle self-consciousness!

> *Your dear and grateful*
> *and mannered friend,*
> *R.L.S.*

Poring over this account, in my room, at night, aptly on the Feast of Saint Cogitosus, I can see where an astute reader would ask, And where is the conflict? Where is the daily grinding and grating of one nature against another of a wholly different character? Where is dyspepsia and vulgarity and sneer and aggression and covetousness and theft and outright lie? Where is there assault and vengeance, plot and peeve? Where are the marital difficulties and the seething misunderstandings and misapprehensions inherent in any romance worthy of the name? Have we gotten all the way in this account, this report, this memoir, and somehow not encountered distemper, disgruntlement, dislike, disagreeableness, detestation? Could the author be gilding the lily, oiling the troubled waters, closing his eyes to the lewd and crude, the rough and tumble, the inarguable threads of greed and violence in the fabric of human nature?

To which I would say, we have survived, in the previous pages, the kidnapping of a boy, a battlefield of immeasurable savagery, the gaunt aftermath of a terrible famine, the death of a great man at sea, and the ordeal of a young woman hiding in the dank hold of a ship for long and awful weeks, as it crossed thousands of miles of pitching and roaring ocean, and even the bitter silence of the two Irish girls Alice and Loretta who refused to speak to each other—has that not been enough for you? Do we require pain in a narrative, for it to be substantial? Do we need to dwell at length in mud, so that cleansing is more enjoyable? I would rather trust my reader to be astute, and gather from hints and intimations the depth and breadth of the story. All I can do is write the bones, and hope that you will enflesh them as you will, from your imagination and experience; all I can do is present Mr and Mrs Carson as I knew them, and ask you to imagine their tones of voice, the grace of their presence, the swirl of their stories far beyond the page, and far beyond my capacity to tell. In a real sense a story is a dream that I am asking you to share, but to dream in your own fashion, and not so much mine; a story is a willing partnership, which you join with a will, or decline; many a book has been flung across the room, as the reader decides to voyage elsewhere, and there is nothing the writer can do but forge ahead, hoping that other readers will join the journey, board the boat, take a room in the same house, and live there for a few days, a week perhaps, until you finish the story, and confront the finality of a blank page, on which any next adventure or tale may begin. More than once, in my own reading, I have wanted the next story to begin on the blank page that limned the conclusion of the one that just delighted me; but even after the best and most riveting and absorbing tales, you must take a breath, and go for a walk, and let it simmer and marinate in your soul, so that if you are lucky, and the story stands the test of years, it sinks deeply into your soul, and becomes thoroughly a part of you; so it is that I am composed in part of Walter Scott, and William Hazlitt, and the glories of the King James Bible; of Montaigne and Cicero, Shakespeare and the sad and glorious Charles Lamb; of Daniel Defoe and Rabbie Burns my headlong countryman, a man I might have been, all fire and song, foolishness and stuttered grace.

But I will give you a little conflict, if it is the grit you need between your teeth today. Mr and Mrs Carson did disagree once a week, about this and that—a boarder's fee, a kitchen girl's beau; which particular oysters to feature for Saturday dinner; and once I saw her grim about the mouth, when he was asked to join a voyage into the Arctic ice, an expedition its organizers swore would be lucrative and remunerative beyond imagination; they came to the house, and laid out their plans by the fire with passion and eloquence, and Mr Carson listened intently, and I saw Mrs Carson grim and unhappy in the kitchen, though she said nothing whatsoever; but then Mr Carson most courteously saw his guests to the door, and said firmly and quietly that he would not be joining them, and it is my belief that he then went into the kitchen and took Mrs Carson in his arms and said that he would never again be parted from her for even a night, did God give him the grace of that wish; but I did not hear those words spoken, if indeed they were, for I had gone upstairs to my attic room, knowing that some scenes must play out without audience or chronicler.

And there were occasional fistfights and brouhahas between and among boarders; and once a month a tart misunderstanding with a tradesman; and twice that I recall Mr Carson was brusque and terse with someone selling something that Mrs Carson had made quite clear she did not desire; and the kitchen girls squabbled and bickered; and a man was murdered on the steps of the Church of Notre Dame des Victoires nearby, slain by his best friend, who waited weeping by the body for the police to take him to prison; we had a death in the house while I was there, a quiet old man who did not wake up one morning, and who was carried tenderly out of the house by the two somber young men who roomed to either side of him; and a small boy on Powell Street was crushed by a wagon. This last tragedy I remember well, for I saw it from my window; by utter chance I glanced up just as the child dashed into the street and the wagon struck him so hard that his body flew clear across the street. I sprinted down the stairs as fast as I could go, but Mrs Carson was there before me, kneeling with his head in her hands, murmuring and crooning to him. It was a Sunday evening, and the police were long in responding to the accident, and it was dusk by the time the boy was taken away. The crowd that had formed almost immediately had gone, and I walked back into the house with Mrs Carson, who was silent; but I remember that her dress was soaked in blood from neck to toe. That night the house did not dine, as I remember, but each resident fended for himself or herself outside, in the matter of meals.

★

We had a birth in the house too, while I was there: a boy, delivered of Ailís, early in the morning of April 17, and christened Donan, after the saint of that day, for Ailís was a devout Catholic, and the saints and angels were quite real to her, and she was conversant with the cherubim and the seraphim—who perhaps knew more than we did about the boy's father, of whom not one word was ever asked or answered, that I heard. Donan the saint I did know, however; while he was Irish, his missionary work was in Scotland, and his name is still spoken with reverence in the northern islands of my native land, particularly on the small island of Eigg. I had been there myself, with my father, when I was a boy, as he examined and charted lighthouses, which was his work as an engineer; that was the work I was to do, he hoped, but I had no interest in engineering, and a fervent interest in stories.

It was on Eigg, I remember, that I had a conversation with my father that was prescient about our future divergence; he talked about how a small lighthouse might be built there, to aid in navigation among the little islands, while I talked about the many stories of Donan: that he had been saying Mass when pirates attacked, and he begged them to let him finish the Mass before he and his fellow monks were all slain, and that they had all been beheaded, or that they had all been locked in their chapel, and burnt to death together, not one of them crying aloud in pain, so as not to afflict his brothers with sadness. I remember being excited, as I told my father these stories, and that when I was done he stared at me with a look on his face I could never find words for, though I have made my way with words ever since. Disappointment, certainly; and a little confusion, that *this* was his only child? And something like dawning sadness, as he began to understand that I would not follow him in the craft that he and his grandfather and father and brothers and nephew loved, and that indeed we shared almost nothing, in the way of passions and convictions. I did not know then, and only can imagine now, the pain of realizing that the child you love with all your heart and soul is a stranger, and perhaps always will be, no matter how many years you both shall live.

I held little Donan in my arms, a week after he was born, a week before I left the house myself, to begin a new life, and I found myself powerfully moved; not so much by the tiny creature in my arms, though he was a serene and handsome lad, as babies go, but by thoughts of fathers. Donan's absent father, not even a myth, not even a name to be cursed and vilified, probably not much more than a boy himself; perhaps he was still in the city, or far away at sea or desert or forest, fleeing what he might think a mistake or a miracle; or perhaps exiled by a bitter Ailís, never even to see his own son. My own father, Thomas Stevenson, proud and honest, stern and amused at once, genial and melancholy by turn, shrewd and boyish, as calm and tempestuous by turns as the sea that absorbed him, and which he fought his whole life; a man who reads only a few books, but those books are deep and wise and he abides in them like a man in a comfortable house; a man who loves all dogs, respects all women, but does not love himself, and holds himself to the most stringent measure, which perforce he cannot meet; so that for all his humor, and his generosity, and his integrity, he sets his face like flint, and I can find no road or path through or around his wall, and this grieves me deeply.

And my own shadow fatherhood; a father in spirit but not in fact; more uncle than father; a father one or two or ten steps removed from the actual task and gift and labor and prayer of it. In a month I will have two children, but I will have no children at all; in a month I will read to a boy and tuck him into his bed, and dine with him, and pore over his schoolbooks, and explore the beach for bones and miracles, and climb trees just because, and draw heroes and saints, and make jokes and snowballs, and listen with ferocious attentiveness to the shiver of his heart and the glimmer of his mind, but I will not be his father, I will never be his father, and will that not always be silently between us, what I am not, rather than whatever it is I am?

★

On the first day of May, as a wedding present for Fanny and me, John Carson borrowed a boat from a friend—a small sloop he told me privately was almost certainly used for oyster piracy, as he could tell from its lines and rigging—and took us sailing in San Francisco Bay. Lloyd was thrilled to go a'sailing, as he said, as was Mary Carson, though she protested she could not, under any circumstances, spare the entire day; but her protest was a form of private theater, I thought—something like the steps of a dance they had invented for themselves, and much enjoyed practicing, as actors sing scales before they go on stage.

John Carson, as you would imagine of an experienced seaman, handled the pretty little boat with a deft ease that was delightful to watch—any artisan at work is a pleasant experience, a lesson in motion and experience and absorption turned to good effect—and though I asked to be of service as crew, I was told politely but firmly that my berth was passenger only, and my duties were to watch over Fanny and Lloyd, and be sure they did not fall overboard, or get overly sick from the rollicking voyage—for *rollick* we did, from one end of the bay to the other, at terrific speed, sometimes clutching each other in trepidation and delight, and shouting at the tops of our voices.

West from Black Rock Cove to the Golden Gate, into the wind, slipping across the bows of bigger ships like a falcon against a cliff face; a turn into Horseshoe Bay and through Raccoon Strait straight and fast as a dart; back south again through the shallows along the eastern shores, looking for crabs and fish, hoping to see a sturgeon; past Oakland, with Lloyd craning to see the cottage, and Fanny and I hanging on to his legs for dear life; and then down to the far south of the bay, poking into coves and inlets, raising flustered and aggrieved herons from their fishing, admiring the diligent osprey and the tireless cormorant. . . .

I do not think I could ever find the proper song of sentences to portray that day, no matter how hard I searched for them, and me a man so desirous to be great at just such pursuit. The rattle of the rigging lines, the cheerful battering of the breezes, the sheer bodily vivacity of rushing through the open air at such a pace, with only the sound of water and wind and merriment as accompaniment; the extraordinary light, surely of a different cast here on the Pacific shore than anywhere else on earth; the quiet joy of being with those we love and those we esteem; and something deeply savory too because it was a gift, freely given, from a friend, indeed two friends, whom I had not known, mere months ago, and now counted among my close companions.

We do not acknowledge enough, I think, the clan and tribe of our friends, who are not assigned to us by blood, or given to us to love by a merciful Creator, but come to us by grace and gift from the mass of men, stepping forth unannounced from the passing multitudes, and into our lives; and so very often stepping right into the inner chambers of our hearts. In so many ways we celebrate those we love as wife or husband, father and mother, brother and sister, daughter and son; but it is our friends whom we choose, and who choose us; it is our friends we turn to abashed, when we are bruised and broken by love and pain; it is our friends whose affection and kindness are food and drink to our spirits, and sustain and invigorate us when we are worn and weary.

It was dusk when we landed again in Black Rock Cove, and John Carson handed the boat over to a smiling man who waved at us but did not speak; and we all five walked along the bayfront to the Oakland ferry, John Carson stopping here and there to speak quietly to men in the shadows. By the time we reached the ferry jetty, Lloyd was sound asleep, aboard the sturdy upper deck of John Carson's shoulders; only when Fanny escorted him gently onto the ferry did he startle awake, and bow sleepily and thank the Carsons, before he instantly fell asleep again. Fanny made her farewells and I mine, and the Carsons and I walked peaceably back to Bush Street through a night of such stars like I had never seen. Since that night I have voyaged deep and wide, and have seen many a sky that made me gape in wonder; but to this day when I think of a starry sky, the memory to mind is that night in May, in rough and salty San Francisco, in those last days I lived on Bush Street.

★

It was clear both to Fanny and myself that we could not live in San Francisco, or Oakland, or in the great green hand of America itself, but that we should head home, first to Scotland and then perhaps to England, or France—somewhere where I could set about my writing seriously and assiduously, armed for the first time with enough money for us not to worry daily and hourly about the roof over our heads and the paucity of bread in the bowl. Fanny was of a mind to paint, and see if she could sell a work here and there, and augment the family finances; Lloyd, already experienced at his tender age in switching from one school to another and one country to another, would be adventurously fine with what would be painful tumult in another boy's life; and Fanny's gentle daughter Isobel was happy here in California with her husband Joe Strong, and was happy too, she said, to see us off and away on journeys, especially as her mother would, as she said, be happy and safe, for the first time, and also cared for and attended to and savored, none of which she had felt before from a husband.

First we would pause in Napa Valley, and perhaps Sonoma, and enjoy a honeymoon on a hill, in a ranch house high above Calistoga, up above the mists, in God's own sunlight, in which I planned to bask, mumbling happily and incoherently, for days at a time, with a cutlass for rattlesnakes, and not a care else in the world; but then away to Edinburgh, to present the new Mrs. Stevenson to her new in-laws, and to introduce my estimable father and mother to their new grandson; it tells you something deep of my parents' characters that I *knew* they would gather both Fanny and Lloyd into their hearts, no matter how unusual the manner of their arrival into our clan. As flinty as my father could be, as stern and righteous and strict about moral matters, he understood very well that the essence of the faith he loved with all his heart was finally humility and tenderness; beyond even justice there is mercy, as so many staunch fathers of the church forget, in their rush to protect and define and expand the monument built upon the broken body of that poor young Judean, all those centuries ago. But it is His message, not His monument, that marks the true faith, and celebrates the trace of his strange genius.

So it was that May was a flurry of packing and repacking, of closing up the cottage and closing up affairs, of arranging this and rearranging that. I finished all my loose manuscripts, and shipped them off to Sidney Colvin in London, to shepherd and sell as he saw fit, with the proceeds, if any, to be held for my eventual arrival. My own scanty possessions were boxed up and ready in an hour, being mostly quills and notebooks, two pairs of boots, my Bible and my Plutarch, my *Kilmarnock* and my *Rob Roy*—no Scotsman leaves his native land without Walter Scott and Rabbie Burns for his close companions—and my inviolate memories of that tiny wooden room, that swaying mast of a house, that brawny bustling city, that vast California of dense fog and sharp light.

And of my landlady and her husband. I had come to realize, in my last days in the house, that they had become such
dear and close friends, that parting would be wrenching; to
think that never again would I listen to John Carson by the
fire, or to Mrs Carson in the kitchen, shucking oysters, was
terribly sad. In so many ways they had welcomed me into
their home and into their hearts, and given a foreign wraith
such a harbor as he had never dreamed possible, half a world
from his own home, and weak with illness, and as close to
penniless as a man can come, and still have a scrap of pride.

Here in their house I had done good work; here in their city
I would be married; here in their state I had been welcomed
by children soon to be my own; here in their gracious company I had been thrilled by stories from all over the world, by
remarkable adventures and expeditions and voyages more
wonderful than I could tell in a hundred books, and met
their fascinating friends. But here in this house, more than
anything, I had been given good friends and true. In whatever years that are left to me, whenever I hear the words "San
Francisco," those salty windy misty hilly words, I will instantly see John and Mary Carson, the one meditating by the
fire in his best frock coat, and the other poking her head in
from the kitchen, as redolent tendrils of dinner slip past her,
to call gently for the man she loves, the man she crossed the
world to find. For they did cross half the world each, to retrieve the other, though they could not have explained the
powerful yearning then, and cannot even now; but I can mar-

vel at it, as their friend, as a student of wonderful stories, and as a man who himself crossed half the world to claim his love, against all advice and sense. But if ever a human construct ought to be viewed with the most withering suspicion at all times, it is that which we call sense; which is quite often only the frontier of our imagination, sometimes a prison wall we erect around ourselves, fearful of what is beyond.

★

Every day now was a last day, and I savored every moment, every detail, every drop. One last night I shucked oysters in the kitchen, and listened to Mary Carson tell me about the little man in Montreal, who sent her tiny bottles of oil from the lamps around his beloved statue of Saint Joseph; she used the oil with the sick in her house, and accounted it miraculous sometimes, depending on the willingness of the patient to believe it so. One last day I walked up Pine Street from the waterfront, and felt the city begin to rise under my feet at Kearny, and watched with a throng of fellow amazed souls as Andrew Hallidie's new cable car ran up the hill, its passengers fearful and delighted. The long slow climb to Nob Hill, a moment to rest at Powell, and then uphill again to Mason, where the city crests; once again I pass by Hyde Street, and think that Hyde would be a lovely name for a character in a novel; once again, for the hundredth time since I arrived in this city after Christmas, I revel in the scents and airs of the trees—olive and avocado, lime and lemon, the sharp spice of eucalyptus—I think that I could pick that brisk commanding scent of a thousand, and know it to be the most Californian scent of all—along with money and wine, I suppose, and the faint bronze smell of dreams.

To the Presidio, and beyond it the wild windy whip of the Golden Gate; past all the old stone churches, tall and proud and nodding politely to their cousins; around every corner and through every lane and alley, still discovering new views of the sea and bay, even after so many miles of perambulation; through ten, twenty, thirty languages hailing from every corner of the world; past faces of every cast and color imaginable, from pale to pink, brown to black, russet to ruddy; past horses and dogs and supercilious cats; mules and burros and here and there still a cow, quietly munching the neighbor's roses; once an amused parrot aboard a sailor's shoulder; and once the tiniest monkey I have ever seen, atop a soldier, and looking very much like a bright-eyed hat.

And one last night I sat with John Carson, and listened to him sail the world, tacking always toward his Mary, drawn by some volition he could not name. One last night he told me stories—of Australia, in which he had wandered deep into the northern wilderness, and come upon a tribe that loved chess and played it brilliantly, and played a ritual living chess game every year when the rains came, the women against the men, the pieces dressed in feathers and crocodile skins, moving at the command of chiefs on a hill, who issued their instructions by running children; sweet it was, said John Carson, to watch a small boy, naked but for a belt of parrot feathers, lead his mother by the hand from one place to another, at which point applause for the grace of the move would fill the valley.

Of Canada, where he and his shipmate, as they wandered Vancouver Island, had rescued a shriveled bear from a pit, and restored it to health with salmon and berries, and been rewarded with an elk calf, carried by the bear to their very campfire; *there* was a moment to remember all your life, said Mr Carson, my mate and I sitting astonished as the bear placed her thanks at our feet, and we all stared at each other a long moment, with much being said without words being necessary, and then she faded back into the forest.

Of the death of his dear friend Gurumarra at sea near the Navigator Islands, and how and why that had happened, Gurumarra leaping overboard in a storm, and holding up a shipmate overcome by the sea, and then sinking away himself into the depths, with no corpse to be found, though the ship waited there all the next day, in reverence and grief— "Every one of us," said John Carson, "every one of us, captain included, for there was a man admired by all, and mourned with piercing sadness; I do not think any one of us from that ship ever fully recovered ourselves from that loss, though I am the only one who believes I will see him again somehow, in whatever form we assume in the next life; it was Gurumarra who assured me that who we are persists past who we were, and he was not a man for fanciful belief or religious claptrap. If he told you a thing was so, it was incontrovertibly so, whether you understood it or not."

And many more stories—of a nearly deaf boy in New

South Wales named Henry, whom Mr Carson was sure would someday be that country's Mark Twain; of a man he met in Ireland, who scoured the ditches and swales of County Mayo for the bones of those who had starved alone and unremarked, and buried their bones in boxes shaped like boats; of a hawk he had known in Scotland, which could read, and answer questions by writing in the dirt with a talon; of a magical book he had been shown once in Wales, which filled itself with different stories according to ideas of its own, and one time would be an adventure, and the next a treatise on philosophy, and yet again a manual about the cultivation of oats.

I think I will always remember that last night by the fire—for so many reasons. It was the apex and culmination of so many other nights like it, swirling with story, with Mr Carson's quiet voice tendrilling out of the flickering firelight, carrying us around the world; such an ancient habit and joy, telling stories by the fire! How many thousands and hundreds of thousands of years have human beings sat, rapt and riveted, our imaginations thrilling, as a voice came out of the darkness carrying seas and ships, mountains and men, forests and fights, loss and love? And it ended with Mr Carson's voice shivering a bit, as he said that he too had much enjoyed our hours here by the hearth, and would remember them always with pleasure, even as I went on to what he was sure would be a famous career, for he thought that stories would come to me always, trusting me to tell them honestly, with both verve and humility, trying to tell them well, but not taking overmuch credit for the way in which they were drawn to my imagination like metal to magnet; some people, like you and Mr Clemens, are *seanachies,* as Mrs Carson says in the Irish—storycatchers, born to hear and share stories, a holy craft, in the end.

And too he asked me quietly, before we parted, to carry Mrs Carson particularly in my heart, and pray for her in whatever way was most comfortable for me; for she was newly with child, and it might be that the prayers of a dear friend, for that is how he and Mrs Carson thought of me, would help steer the child safely through its long voyage in the sea of its mother, and arrive safe in the harbor of her arms at last. To this I said yes with all my heart; and that night I knelt and prayed as I had not done since I was a child in stormy Scotland, kneeling by my thin bed in that tiny wooden room at the top of the ship on Bush Street.

★

Does every man remember every moment of his wedding day, so that years later he can close his eyes and return there in an instant, thrilled and nervous, and buffing his boots for the ninth time? I suspect so, I suspect so; for I am only one man, but every instant of that one day has remained resident in me as clear and vibrant as the day itself; I can call it up with the snap of a finger, and often I do so in lazy moments, for the sheer pleasure of it; Fanny has caught me smiling secretly, and taxes me cheerfully for living in the past. But to me it is not past, that delicious day, and I live it over again every morning, even now, when I awake, and there she is, *my wife*; the most remarkable words I know, and me a professional herder and recruiter of words, surrounded by them all day long and into the night.

I buffed my boots that morning, again and again; I paced my room, now empty of all my papers and pens and books, all packed for our honeymoon; I smoked a dozen cigarettes; I said farewell to the ebullient sparrows who had haunted my windowsill, and sometimes hopped into the room, and leapt about looking for crumbs; I stared out one last time at the sprawling city below my wooden tower, the city that had hosted me these riveting months, that had offered me stories and friends and clean salt air, and God alone knows how many oysters; and I went downstairs for the last time.

I confess it here that I paused often along the way, running my hand slowly along the shining old banister, gazing with foolish affection on the doors of the other boarders, taking a strange pleasure in the sheer familiarity of the creaking planks along the staircase, especially the one with divots from a logger's boots, who came home in his cups one night, and dreamed he was in a log-rolling contest. Mr Carson had told me he had many times bent to replace that board, but never did so, as the pitted surface continually reminded him of the logger, "a good man, a kind man, and a wonderful log-roller, too, twice champion of the state of Oregon," as he said with a smile.

Past the drawing room, and the fireplace so often flanked by two slouched men and four long legs, aswirl with smoke from cigarette and cigar; past the oysterous kitchen, the scullery, the pantry, the mudroom, the wood-room, the back porch as rigged with lines and set with sheets as any ship at sea, though the house sails were for sleep and the ship's for speed. And then finally to the long narrow hallway lined with prints and engravings of the sea, and paintings of Achill and Montreal, and hung with the most amazing arcana, from a bear trap to a crucifix carved of walrus tusk; not an inch of that hallway was without adornment, it seemed to me, and I had many times pored the walls, each and every time finding some new detail I had not noticed before.

But this one last time down the hallway I had no eyes for the works on the walls, for the hall was lined with smiling people, and as I stood there agape they reached for me, and clapped me on the back, and pumped my hand energetically, and handed me small gifts of one kind or another (including an imposing clasp-knife, I discovered later), and beamed at me so warmly that I was overwhelmed, and came very near tears. Mrs Carson saw this, and made a brief speech about how it had been a pleasure and an honor to have me as a guest in her house, a pleasure because I was a gentleman and treated everyone with kindness and generosity, and an honor because I was surely destined to be a great and unforgettable author, and the fact that I had lived at 608 Bush Street would go down in history forever, and someday probably there would be a plaque on the wall outside, probably with her name misspelled. This got a burst of laughter, in which I recovered myself, and Mr Carson led me down the steps onto Bush Street.

Up Bush Street one last time, past Notre Dame des Victoires, where the bells pealed resoundingly just as we walked past, causing us to laugh; over busy Powell and Mason streets, past taverns and shops of every stripe, past an ostler and a cobbler, past teams of horses, past a disconsolate donkey, past children of every shade of skin imaginable. It seemed to me that morning that I saw and felt and heard and smelled every grain of the fabric of the city, every redolence and stench, every cry and screech and song, as crisp and clear as if it were my first day there, perhaps because it was my last, and all of my senses were at their full pitch, to carry away as much of the city as possible.

Underfoot the stone and wood, mud and scuff, cobble and duff, and here and there the naked ancient hill itself; I fancied once that I saw an aboriginal footprint in the dust, left long ago by a Miwok maid. Overhead crows and jays, and an occasional gull—that piercing shout is the sound I most associate with San Francisco, even though I have heard it slicing through the moist air of maritime cities from Scotland to Samoa. Down Taylor Street now, past Sutter Street, past an alley filled

with swallows, darting and whirling in the most amazing fashion; perhaps there was a cloud of insects trapped there somehow, and the swallows were gorging as seabirds gorge on mobs of bait-fish, but perhaps it was a convocation of swallows for reasons of their own, gathered in an alley holy to them, or one housing a great queen of their clan, now reborn as a girl child; who knows the ways of the world's other beings, for all our confidence that we hold dominion over them? And finally to Post Street, and the minister's house; where, waiting for us in a great room by the fireplace, I found my Fanny, and very soon after I took her hand in mine, we were married at last.

It would entail another whole book, or a series of them, to tell the story aright, of that beaming day, let alone our next three lazy delicious days at the Palace Hotel, and then our voyage north across the bay to Napa Valley, where we honeymooned high on a hill amid madrone and manzanita, and rattlesnakes and the most wonderful hot reviving nutritious sun; I do not think I have ever been so happy and healthy as I was those weeks in Silverado, nor do I think I have ever seen Fanny more relaxed, before or since that time; I will always have a chapel in my heart for that sunlit hilltop, with its shy deer and bold snakes. To me it was something like the very cupped gracious hand of California, where Fanny and I drank the first draughts of the marriage for which we had waited so long.

Instead let me leave you with a few last images, and let them sketch the story in brief: Isobel embracing me long and hard after the ceremony, and sobbing with some deep mixture of relief and sadness and joy . . . Lloyd holding my hand so tightly the rest of the day that it was all I could do to pry it loose when we tucked him into bed that night . . . the round-faced Reverend Scott beaming as brightly as the moon, and joking about John Calvin's patently odd terror of dancing, what sort of dunderhead could conceivably be afraid of *dancing*? . . . Fanny's own tears of relief and joy in the back garden of the minister's house, to which she had repaired, ostensibly to rehabilitate her hair, blown askew by the usual San Franciscan afternoon gale . . . Mary Carson presenting us with a chess set carved from all the woods of California, so that we would remember that golden land, no matter how far we traveled from it . . . Mrs Carson presenting us also with a gift from Ailís and Éadaoin, which turned out to be pearls for Fanny, found in a crate of oysters sent from Vancouver Island . . . Mr Carson handing me a gift which he said had been mailed to the house a week ago, which turned out to be a copy of Mark Twain's new book, *A Tramp Abroad,* sent without return address, but postmarked Connecticut . . . Fanny's face, as she peered up at me after we had promised our lives to each other, that alert mysterious eager untamed unquenchable face I'd been utterly absorbed by since the first moment I saw it, through a window in a hotel in France . . .

But let me conclude with one last image for you to carry away, here at the end. Imagine a young Scotsman stepping forth to be married to his great love, the woman he adores, the woman he knows in his heart is the partner of his innermost soul, until death do them part; but he does so in a country far from his own, and far from his friends, far even from his father, who might in other circumstances stand as witness for his only son, in the hour of his wedding. Had I been married in Scotland, or England, I might have had my dear friend Colvin stand with me, or my beloved cousin Bob; nor did I have a child myself, to stand with me, as Isobel stood with Fanny. I thought about Lloyd, but did not wish to add more weight to the tumult of his life, and him just eleven years old—better to let the boy enjoy the pomp of the day, and enjoy the prospect not of a new father, but at least of a male companion in the family, who might actually pay attention to him, and play and work with him in his adventures and studies, and give him at the least a steady affection, which he so long had lacked.

No, not Lloyd; but there *was* a man here in San Francisco I much admired, and counted now as a dear friend; a man I hoped to be in correspondence with the rest of my days, a man I trusted, a man who would, I knew for a fact, care for my family, should I be removed from life betimes; and that is the man I asked to stand as witness with me on the day Fanny and I were married on Post Street. He wore his best black suit, John Carson did, and the very boots he had worn on his adventures in several quarters of the world. Worn as they were, they shone with polishing—Ailís and Éadaoin had both had at them, and Mr Carson had attacked them himself twice that morning with barrels of bootblack, as he said—and he told me later that in his opinion they were now composed more of polish than of boot, and that a stiff afternoon breeze off the bay would reduce and scatter them like sand.

When I think of the day that Fanny married me, I think of many things, all of them rich and pleasurable and moving; foremost among them Fanny's face, in that first moment after our vows, and the desperate happiness with which Lloyd gripped my hand all afternoon and evening. But then I remember, with the deepest pleasure, that such a man as John Carson stood beside me as my companion and witness at that sweetest of moments; and that after I had kissed Fanny, and embraced Isobel, and shaken hands gravely with Lloyd, it was to John Carson that I turned, and, taking his big rough hand, expressed, as well as I could, my most sincere and heartfelt gratitude for his kindness, his generosity, and his friendship. We are all travelers in this world, and the best we can find in our travels is an honest friend; I found such a man one winter and spring in San Francisco, and I hope that in telling you something of his remarkable adventures, I have told you something deeper of his even more remarkable character.

Afterword

The reader who is interested in the life and work of the remarkable Robert Louis Stevenson (and who would not be
absorbed by such a riveting and gracious soul?) can plunge
happily into all sorts of excellent biographies, studies, and
books by RLS; beyond his four masterpieces (the novels *Treasure Island, Kidnapped,* and *Jekyll and Hyde,* and the irresistible
charm of *A Child's Garden of Verses*), I particularly recom-
mend his later essays (my favorite is a collection called *The
Lantern-Bearers & Other Essays*), his great book of horror stories *The Merry Men,* his South Seas novella *The Beach of
Falesa,* and his half-finished final novel *Weir of Hermiston,*
which I think might have been a fifth masterpiece, had he
lived to complete it; he died on the evening of December 3,
1894, of stroke, after dictating some of *Weir* to Fanny's
daughter Isobel, whom he loved as his own child. He was
only forty-four years old, poor soul. *Fifth masterpiece,* by the
way, is an amazing phrase—few human beings are allowed
to write one masterpiece, let alone four and a half. My favorite biography of him is his cousin Graham Balfour's *Life*

of Robert Louis Stevenson, and a perceptive modern profile is Philip Callow's *Louis.* But I might suggest that you will find more of the man in books by him than about him; dip into *Kidnapped* again, or read *Treasure Island* for the first time since you were a youth, and *there* is the man, cheerful and dashing and eloquent and delighted to be alive and telling stories.

It is probably worth noting here that his plays, and his novels written with his stepson Lloyd, are *not* very good, which makes me like him all the more; for one thing, he devoted many hours to writing books with his stepson, which is a cool and generous thing to do with your time if you are a genius, and shows us his character, and also it's refreshing that he was not great at everything; if he was a master of *all* literary forms we would dislike him a little, I suspect, from envious awe.

The basic facts in the previous pages are true: Stevenson did indeed live with the Carsons on Bush Street, from December 1879 to late March or early April of 1880 (the plaque on Bush Street today, commemorating his residence there, claims that he left in March, but I find no evidence that he did so, and have preferred to leave him with the Carsons until his wedding day), and he and Fanny did marry on May 19, in San Francisco, at the home of the Reverend Doctor William Anderson Scott, a Presbyterian minister. Their friend Dora Williams suggested to the newlyweds that they honeymoon in the hills above Napa, an experience that led to Stevenson's delightful honeymoon memoir *The Silverado Squatters.* I have happily placed John and Mary Carson at the wedding, because how could they possibly not be there, and who now is to say they were not?

John Carson's friend Alfred Russel Wallace was indeed a world-famous scientist and veteran of the jungles of Borneo. Wallace conceived the theory of natural selection wholly independently of Charles Darwin, and in fact Wallace's artless letter to Darwin about his thoughts led directly to Darwin hurriedly finishing and publishing his epic *The Evolution of Species* for fear that he would be trumped as to the origins of his remarkable perceptions. That the two men became good friends of great mutual esteem is a compliment to their great generosity of spirit. Wallace was also a fine writer (he is much more fun to read than Darwin, I think), and I relish, and have much leaned on here, his great book *The Malay Archipelago.*

The Catholic priest who served with John Carson in the War Between the States was also a real and fascinating man: the Reverend William Corby, of the Congregation of Holy Cross, the order affiliated most famously in America with the University of Notre Dame, in Indiana. Corby did serve with the famous Irish Brigade (Sixty-ninth New York Infantry, whose battle roar was *fág an bealach,* Gaelic for "clear the way"), did famously stand on a rock at Gettysburg before the slaughter in the wheat field, and did offer absolution to the men (he said later that the prayer was meant for men on both sides, not just the North), and surely he must have wept in horror at the ensuing carnage. He was later twice named president of the University of Notre Dame, and there are statues commemorating his extraordinary moment on the rock both at Gettysburg and at Notre Dame, which also named its priests' residence hall for him. Readers particularly interested in the history of the Irish Brigade ought to read Tim Egan's terrific *The Immortal Irishman,* and after that read Egan's other books, particularly *The Worst Hard Time.* That man is a fine writer and no mistake.

The small intense man in Montreal who was so kind to Mary Carson in her flight across Canada was also quite real, and also a member of the Congregation of Holy Cross: he is now called Saint Andre Bessette, after his canonization in 2010 by Pope Benedict XVI. An altogether fascinating man, he was by many accounts grumpy, testy, tiny, illiterate, rude—and legendarily credited with hundreds of miraculous cures effected through his intercession, especially with Saint Joseph. Brother Andre (he was not a priest) himself constantly and rudely refused credit for the efficacy of his prayers. *"Ite ad Joseph!"* he would snarl at those who asked for his help, and by some accounts he would then slam his door in their faces. Yet he apparently spent many hours a day in prayer, he was the irrefutable force who led to Saint Joseph's Oratory being built on Mount Royal, and he is still, long after his death in 1937, credited with miracles; witness the room filled with abandoned crutches and canes today at the oratory.

Robert Louis Stevenson did indeed have a friend named Captain Anson Smith, who did run a goat ranch in Carmel, and was a bear hunter; Colonel John Fremont's troops in the Bear Flag revolt and the later war against Mexico for

California were so ragtag (and Fremont such a greedy schemer wholly disinterested in channels of authority and organization) that no one knows if Smith was formally a captain or not; but Stevenson called him one, and so we will take that as gospel.

The abandoned stone village on Sliabh Mór on Achill Island, the Island of the Eagles, is quite real, and still there, and I have seen it, and it is still, to my mind, haunted and extraordinary and sad. My particular thanks here to my dear friend Michael Patrick Mulcrone of County Mayo, who brought me to Achill and showed me much of that holy and mysterious Irish island, from which, I note happily, the ancestors of the terrific American novelist Alice McDermott came. More homework: read McDermott's Irish American masterpieces *Charming Billy* and *Someone*.

The ship *Duke of Sutherland* arrived in Sydney Harbor on February 4, 1879, after a voyage from London; listed among the four "ordinary seamen," the lowest ranking aboard, was a very young Conrad de Korzeniowski, better known later by his pen name Joseph Conrad. I have leaned a bit on Conrad's memoirs, *The Mirror of the Sea* and *A Personal Record,* for the flavor and tenor of his talk, and also, of course, like any sensible reader, swum thoroughly in his novels. Conrad may well be the one writer I know who never wrote a lesser novel. I love his sea novels, but his land novels are superb. Remarkable man. Imagine becoming one of the greatest of writers in a language that is the *third* you learned; he grew up speaking Polish and French.

Mark Twain, still toggling back and forth between the names Sam Clemens and Mark Twain, did indeed live in San Francisco in 1865 and 1866, and did write hilariously about dogs and earthquakes and charlatans and mountebanks, and did indeed publish *A Tramp Abroad* in 1880, a very funny and perceptive book, which I assign to you as homework, right after you read his masterpieces *The Adventures of Tom Sawyer, Life on the Mississippi,* and *Roughing It.* (*Huck Finn* is almost a masterpiece, but Twain totally lost the narrative thread at the end, and the book slumps to a bedraggled conclusion; Twain himself clearly lost interest, and just wanted to be done with the thing, a great shame; a good editor could have saved that book, and it might today be in the discussion of Greatest American Novel Ever, with *To Kill a Mockingbird* and *The Great Gatsby.*) Twain, by the way, apparently did *not* actually say "the coldest winter I ever spent was a summer in San Francisco," but it's a great line, and if anyone *would* have said it, surely it would have been Twain. I note with fascination that Twain and Stevenson had the highest regard for each other's work, and did finally meet each other, on a bench one April day in Washington Square in New York City, where they spent hours in conversation; no one knows what they said (each man referred only briefly to their time together), but I, of course, being a Twain and Stevenson nut, happily tried to re-create the whole five hours; see "Sam and Louis" in the Summer 2014 issue of *The Georgia Review.*

The last line in the book is drawn from Robert Louis Stevenson himself, from the introduction to his charming book *Travels with a Donkey in the Cevennes,* one of the first great travel books: "But we are all travellers in what John Bunyan calls the wilderness of this world—all, too, travellers with a donkey: and the best that we find in our travels is an honest friend. He is a fortunate voyager who finds many. We travel, indeed, to find them. They are the end and the reward of life. They keep us worthy of ourselves. . . . Of what shall a man be proud, if he is not proud of his friends?"

Stevenson's closest friend (to whom he dedicated *Travels with a Donkey*) was Sidney Colvin, a literary critic of wit and perception and for many years the print and engravings curator at the British Museum; they met when Stevenson was twenty-two and were instantly the best of friends, remaining so until Stevenson's death in 1894. "I have known no man," wrote Colvin in 1896, "in whom the poet's heart and imagination were combined with such a brilliant strain of humour and such an unsleeping alertness and adroitness of the critical intelligence. . . . His perceptions and emotions were acute and vivid in the extreme . . . to his ardent fancy the world was a theatre glowing with the lights and bustling with the incidents of romance. To find for all he had to say words of vital aptness and animation—to communicate as much as possible of what he has somewhere called 'the incommunicable thrill of things'—was from the first his endeavour in literature, [and] the main passion of his life. . . ."

Let us conclude there, with that eager amused energetic image of Robert Louis Stevenson in our minds; for this book is, in a real sense, a song of him and his spirit, and to the avid tender "thrill of things" that lives in every heart. Rest in peace, brother, on your Samoan mountain. Millions of us still read you, and I suspect you will be read with respect and affection and awe as long as there are human beings absorbed by story; which I hope will be forever.

Thanks & Notes

I leaned heavily and steadily on two books in particular, in recounting the adventures of John Carson: *From Scotland to Silverado,* by Robert Louis Stevenson, in an edition edited by James Hart, and *The Selected Letters of Robert Louis Stevenson,* edited by Ernest Mayhew, a thorough and deft distillation of what I think might be RLS at his very best, funny and tart-tongued and honest and genuine.

I also owe a debt to several writers and friends who, I have discovered with delight over the years, are also mad Stevenson fans, and join me in loving the verve and energy and depth of his work; their cheerful notes and encouragement were a great boon to me, and made me laugh, and in substantive ways made me think a book like this actually ought to be attempted by the least among us. So to America's Cynthia Ozick, Australia's Helen Garner, and the planet's Pico Iyer, I bow in thanks.

While we are on the subject of great writers who love Stevenson's work, it's interesting to note how many of the world's best writers esteemed Stevenson and thought him one of the finest writers ever: Mark Twain, Jorge Luis Borges, Henry James, G. K. Chesterton. If many of the finest writers past and present think a writer is one of the finest writers ever, could he be one of the finest writers ever? Just asking.

I also leaned on a number of other helpful books: Ross Slotten's fine biography of Alfred Russel Wallace, *The Heretic in Darwin's Court*; Wallace's own terrific *The Malay Archipelago*, first published in 1869; *Old Achill Island*, by Hugh Oram; *Achill Island: The Deserted Village at Slievemore*, by Bob Kingston; *An Irish Country Childhood*, by Marrie Walsh; and *San Francisco Bay*, by Harold Gilliam.

Also I must here thank the genius Joseph Conrad; not only do I love and regularly swim again in the best of his work, but surely much of the pleasure of imagining John Carson's voice unspooling stories from his shadowy corner near the fire was born forty years ago when I first savored (in a glorious edition called *A Conrad Argosy*) how Conrad's sailor Charles Marlow narrates *Lord Jim, Chance, Heart of Darkness*, and the terrific story "Youth." For your homework assignment tomorrow, read "Youth." Conrad at his very best is mesmerizing.

My thanks also to Lee Brenneisen and Gerald Asher and Michael Miller, who have shown me much of their beloved San Francisco; to my friend Micheál Pádraic Mulcròin, who first brought me to Achill Island; and to the great Australian journalists James Button and Martin Flanagan, who have been most trustworthy sources of their country's history and literature for me. And finally my quiet prayers for the soul of Harriette McDougall, whose honest gentle memoir of her years in Borneo taught me much of that place and that time. *Sketches of Our Life at Sarawak,* published in 1882 by the Society for Promoting Christian Knowledge in London, is now available free on Project Gutenberg.